Review Copy

This advance review edition of *The Used and Abused* (Part One) by Robert Armin consists of the first 26 out of 45 chapters and an Epilogue that comprise the novel *Oonizhyenniye i oskorblyenniye (The Insulted and Injured)* by Fyodor M. Dostoyevsky, upon which this faithful adaptation has been based. Part Two of *The Used and Abused* will be published in the Fall of 2015.

The Used and Abused
(Part One)

The Used and Abused
(Part One)

Fyodor Dostoyevsky's
The Insulted and Injured
Retold

by
Robert Armin

MORECLACKE PUBLISHING
New York City

Printed in the United States of America

First Edition

Library of Congress Control Number: 2014909539
Moreclacke Publishing, New York, NY

ISBN-13: 978-0996016919

ISBN-10: 0996016910

For Kristine

Principal Characters

Ivan Petrovich, the narrator (called "Vanya")

Nikolai Sergeich Ichmenyev, landowner of Ichmenyevka, facing financial ruin in a lawsuit with Valkovsky

Anna Andreyevna Ichmenyev, his wife

Natalia Nikolayevna Ichmenyev, his daughter (called "Natasha")

Prince Peter Alexandrovich Valkovsky, landowner of Vassilyevskoe

Alexey Petrovich Valkovsky (called "Alyosha"), Valkovsky's impressionable and easily influenced son

Katerina Fedorovna Filimonova, Alexey's wealthy young fiancée (called "Katya")

Jeremiah Smith, an old man

Elena, Mr. Smith's 13-year-old granddaughter (called "Nellie")

Philip Philippich Masloboyev, Vanya's old friend

Alexandra Semyonovna, Masloboyev's sweetheart

Madame Bubnova, a whorehouse Madame and low-life

Princess K., Alexey's godmother, a wealthy dowager

Count Nainsky, a wealthy aristocrat and patron to young Alexey

Countess Zinaida Filimonova, Katya's stepmother

Matreyna, the Ichmenyev's housekeeper

Mavra, Natasha's housekeeper

CHAPTER ONE

Last year, on the evening of March 22nd, I was involved in a very bizarre incident. I had been searching around the city all day looking for a new apartment. Mine was damp and I'd caught a bad cold there. I had wanted to move since the previous autumn, but had put off making the change until then, in the early spring. I'd been searching about, as I said, all day, but found nothing suitable. Above all else, I wanted my new home to be isolated from other people. If necessary, one room would do, but it had to be spacious and, at the same time, I didn't want to pay a lot of rent.

I've always observed that in a confined space one's ideas do not flow freely. I like to pace up and down a room as I meditate upon my novels. And while I'm on the subject of my novels, I confess that I've always found far more pleasure in dreaming them up than in writing them down. Why is that, I wonder, for I'm by no means lazy by nature?

I had been feeling poorly since early that morning and as evening approached I felt even worse. I was feverish and, after having been on my feet all day, extraordinarily tired when I arrived on Voznesensky Avenue a few minutes before sunset.

I love the March sun in St. Petersburg, especially as it is setting on a calm, pleasant evening. When the weather is frosty, the whole street, inundated with floods of light, bursts into glory in an instant. The houses—grey, yellow or dirty green—suddenly erupt into a fountain of sunbeams and lose their sinister aspect in the blink of an eye. A man's soul lights up, as well, and a cold chill runs through his veins and he wakes with a jolt, as though someone had nudged his elbow. New ideas come with the new light. It's astonishing what power a ray of sunshine has on the human soul!

Meanwhile, the sun had set, the frost was growing sharper and beginning to prickle my nose, the darkness grew deeper and the gas-light streamed from the shop windows. I was passing Mueller's pastry shop, which stood on the opposite side of the street, when I suddenly came to a dead stop as though struck by some presentiment that an extraordinary event was about to take place. I felt a most disagreeable shudder run through me as I observed an old man and his dog moving toward the pastry shop. I am certainly no "mystic" and I have little patience with those who claim powers of divination, but I have observed in my lifetime certain inexplicable circumstances that are difficult to explain. This old man, for example. Why did I feel at the very sight of him that something was about to happen to me quite different from my usual daily experiences? It occurred to me that I was feverish and that one's impressions during illness are often deceptive.

As the old man proceeded toward the shop, he advanced with slow and uncertain steps, moving his limbs without bending them as though they were blocks of wood. He stooped and tapped the stones of the pavement with his cane as he went along. I had seen him before in Mueller's shop and each time he had left a sad, disagreeable impression upon me. In all my life, I had never seen so strange and ridiculous-looking a figure: tall, but with a crooked back; a pale octogenarian face that looked like that of a corpse; a worn-out coat, torn at the seams; a round hat, bruised and broken, which might well have seen twenty years of service, covering his nearly bald head which retained only a few strands of yellowing hair at the base of his neck; his automaton-like movements; all these things were quite shocking to people meeting him for the first time.

It was certainly strange to see this old man slogging through a solitary life, seemingly without a soul to look after him, looking more than anything else like a madman who had escaped from his attendants. His leanness was quite beyond description. He had, one might almost say, no body left at all; he was skin and bones and nothing more. His eyes, large but dim and surrounded by deep bluish circles, stared constantly straight in front of him, undeviating. They never looked to the left or the right and never seemed to see anything. I am quite sure of that, for more than once I had noticed that he could stare straight at you and walk straight into you, just as though he had seen nothing but empty space before him.

He had lately begun to frequent Mueller's, he and his dog, but none of the regular customers had ever dared to speak to him and the old man had never said a word to any of them.

"Why does he come to Mueller's?" I thought to myself as I watched him from the other side of the street, unable to take my eyes off of him. "What does he come to do?" I was conscious of a sort of spiteful feeling against him developing in my heart, the consequence, most likely, of illness and fatigue. "What does he think about?" I wondered. "What ideas could he have inside that head? Does he still think at all?" There seemed to be no expression left in that ancient face of his. And where had he found this wretched old dog that appeared to be such an integral and inseparable extension of her master, whom she so closely resembled? This unfortunate animal seemed to be eighty years old, like her master, and looked like no other dog that had ever lived. I don't know why, but the very first time I saw her I imagined that this dog was a beast of some unique species; that she had within her some sort of sorcery; that she was a kind of Mephistopheles in canine form, and that her destiny was in some way or other linked with that of her master by a mysterious tie. She was as thin as a skeleton, or to put it better, as thin as her master. If you had seen this beast you would have thought, as I did, that she had not touched food for years. She was quite bald; her tail stuck to her body like a piece of wood and was pressed tight between her emaciated legs; and her long ears, along with the rest of her head, drooped sadly toward the pavement. In all my life I had never seen a more wretched-looking beast.

When the pair of them walked along the streets, the master in front followed by his dog, her nose glued to the skirts of his coat, their gait and appearance seemed to be crying out with every step, "Oh, but we're old, we're old, oh God, but we're old!"

One day the idea struck me that the old man and his dog had become detached from a page of *Hoffmann's Tales*, illustrated by Paul Gavarni, and that they toured the world as a sort of walking advertisement.

I crossed the road and went into the pastry shop. The old man's behavior inside was equally bizarre and Mueller, from behind his counter, always made an expression of disgust whenever this unwelcome visitor arrived. This singular customer never ordered anything but would go straight to a chair in the corner near the stove and sit. If this chair happened to be occupied, he would stand before the occupant and stare vacantly with a stupid, perplexed look for a few moments and then shuffle off with a disappointed air to the other side of the room near the window. There he would take a chair, seat himself slowly, take off his hat and put it near him on the floor. He would then place his cane alongside his hat, lean full length against the back of his chair and so remain, like a marble statue, for three or four hours at a time. No one had ever seen him with a newspaper in his hand or heard him say a word or even utter a sound.

He used to sit there staring fixedly before him with his dull, lusterless eyes, so that one would readily wager that he neither saw nor heard anything of what was going on around him. His dog, after turning around two or three times in place, would lie down at his feet, gloomy and dejected, push her nose tightly between her master's boots, give a profound sigh and then stretch out full-length on the floor where she would lie immovable, as though she had ceased to live, the whole evening. Anyone might well imagine that these two vampiric creatures, long since dead, were in the habit of resuscitating themselves at sunset solely in order to come to Mueller's shop to fulfill some mysterious obligation unknown to man.

When he had sat like this for some hours, the old man would get up, take his hat and cane, and start towards home. The old dog would get up too, head bent low and tail between her legs, and mechanically follow her aged master.

Most of Mueller's regular customers were Germans, owners of the various establishments on Voznesensky Avenue; a locksmith, a baker, a tailor. Mueller would often approach his guests at their tables and sit with them for a while. He greeted most visitors, including dogs and small children, with great warmth and high spirits. There was a most welcome feeling of camaraderie among the occupants of the shop and visitors were free to play cards, listen to the music, or simply read one of the German newspapers which Mueller kept on hand. I was in the habit of visiting Mueller's on the first day of each month to read the Russian magazines which he also made available. Without exception, everyone in the shop did their best to avoid the old man and they made every effort to sit anywhere but near him in order to show him their disapproval, but he never took the slightest notice of them.

When I went into the shop on this particular evening, I found the old man already installed near the window. His dog, as usual, was stretched out at his feet. I sat down quietly in a corner and wondered, "Why do I come here where I have absolutely nothing to do, especially now when I'm sick and would be much better off going straight home, having a cup of tea and crawling into bed? Have I come here with no other purpose than to study this old man?" A feeling of revulsion seemed to have taken possession of me. "What have I got to do with this old wretch, or he with me?" I remembered the feeling of uneasiness he had caused me in the street. What was this strange compulsion of mine that focused in on every little unimportant event that occurred, and yet kept me from actually observing what was going on around me? A compulsion which one critic who had reviewed my last novel (and who was himself a thinker) had observed and pointed out.

These uneasy thoughts continued to trouble me as I sat there, the weight of illness falling heavier and heavier upon me, until at last I felt that I could not leave this warm room without a greater risk to my health. So I took up a French newspaper, read a few lines, and dozed off.

The Germans in the room, talking about Frankfurt or smoking or reading, did not disturb me, but after about thirty minutes I suddenly woke up, shivering. "I'd better get home," I thought. But a silent pantomime that was taking place in the shop at that moment prevented me from leaving.

I have already mentioned that the old man, as soon as he had settled himself in a chair, would fix his eyes upon some point or other and keep them thus fixed for the rest of the evening. It had been my misfortune, on several occasions, to have this stupidly obstinate gaze (which saw nothing) focused upon me. It was a very uncomfortable, even eerie sensation, and I would usually change my place as quickly as possible.

For the last quarter of an hour the victim of this gaze was a small, neat and plump German, whose red face was encircled by a stiffly starched collar. He was a merchant from Riga, staying in St. Petersburg, whose name, as I learned afterwards, was Adam Ivanich Schultz, and he was an intimate friend of Mueller's. Not yet knowing anything about the old man, he was drinking a toddy and reading *The Village Barber*, when suddenly, raising his head to take a sip of his punch, he observed the old man's gaze sharply focused upon him.

Adam Ivanich was a particularly sensitive man, as are all Germans of the "better" class, and he found it both offensive and insulting to be stared at in so rude a manner. With barely suppressed indignation, he turned his eyes away from this ill-mannered neighbor, muttered something under his breath, and hid behind his book.

Moments later he peered out again and was met by the same obstinate look in the old fellow's eyes and the same utter absence of intelligence in his stare. Adam Ivanich still kept quiet. But the third time his patience gave way and he felt that he must stand up for his dignity and not permit the fair city of Riga (of which he no doubt felt himself the representative) to be compromised in the presence of such distinguished company. He slammed his book onto the table with a loud bang, after which, carried away by his sense of compromised dignity and diminished self-esteem, he fixed his tiny inflamed eyes upon the cause of his displeasure. It looked like a contest as to which one would overcome the other by the magnetic force of his gaze, as though they were waiting to see who would cave in first and admit defeat.

The sound of Adam Ivanich's book hitting the table and the eccentric position in which he had now placed himself quickly focused the attention of everyone present upon the pair. They all stopped what they were doing and looked on with grave and silent curiosity at the two champions. The scene was becoming very comical, but the magnetic attack of Adam Ivanich's stare didn't last long. He turned absolutely crimson, while the old man continued to stare at the furious Mr. Schultz with no more awareness of the onlookers than if they had been on the moon.

Soon Adam Ivanich's patience was completely exhausted and he hollered in German, with a shrill, piercing voice and a threatening air, "Warum starren Sie mich weiterhin so an?" But his adversary seemed to have neither heard nor understood the question and remained silent. So Adam Ivanich decided to speak to him in Russian.

"Why you further stare me in such way?" he screamed with increasing rage, and in very bad Russian, leaping up from his chair.

The old man never moved and the audience murmured its disapproval. Mueller himself, attracted by the noise, entered the room. Upon learning of the circumstances, he judged that the old man was deaf and put his lips close to his ear.

"Herr Schultz has just asked you not to stare at him so obstinately," he said as loudly as he could. The old man slowly turned his gaze upon Mueller and his face, expressionless until this moment, suddenly assumed a look of fear and anxiety. Violently agitated, he stooped and grabbed for his hat and cane, stood up, and with a pitiful smile (the smile of humiliation which a poor man puts on when he has been caught occupying some seat to which he is not entitled and is about to be bodily removed), prepared to go.

There was something so pitiable about this meek and submissive old man's terrified look that touched the heart so deeply that all present, beginning with Adam Ivanich, immediately softened towards him. It was clear that not only was this old man quite incapable of insulting anyone, but that he quite understood that he could be turned out from any place he happened to be in, at any moment, like a beggar. Mueller was a good sort of man and compassionate.

"No, no," he said, patting the old man's shoulder gently to calm him. "Please, sit down again. Herr Schultz, who is an eminent gentleman, well known at Court, has only requested that you not stare at him so, that's all."

But the poor old man understood no more this time than he had before and his agitation only increased. He stooped to pick up a tattered old blue handkerchief that had just fallen out of his hat and called his dog, which was stretched out full length on the floor with her two forefeet pressed against her nose.

"Azor, Azor," he cried in a trembling, broken voice. "Azorka!" But Azorka did not move. She seemed to be asleep. "Azorka," he repeated anxiously, and he touched the dog with the end of his cane, but the dog did not budge. The hat and cane dropped from his grasp as he bent down, fell on his knees and with both hands raised Azor's nose, but there was not the slightest sign of life. Poor Azorka was dead! Dead at her master's feet; of old age, perhaps, or perhaps of starvation.

The old man looked at her for a moment in consternation, as though he did not realize that the dog was dead, and then he stooped quietly over his old servant, his old friend, and pressed his pale face against that of his dead dog. There was a moment of silence. We were all deeply affected. At last, the poor old man got up, his ghastly pallor even whiter than before, and shivered as though under the influence of a terrible fever.

"You could have it stuffed, you know," said Mueller sympathetically, anxious to console the poor old fellow. "It can be stuffed very easily. Fyodor Karlovich Krieger here is a maestro at stuffing animals." Mueller picked up the old man's hat and cane from the floor and returned them to their owner.

"Yes, I know how to stuff animals very well," said Mr. Krieger modestly, coming forward. He was a very tall, thin German, with disheveled red hair and a hooked nose which supported a pair of spectacles.

"Oh yes," added Mueller, growing more enthusiastic over his idea," Fyodor Karlovich Krieger has a wonderful talent for stuffing all sorts of animals."

"Yes, I must say I have some talent for stuffing all sorts of animals," repeated Krieger, "and I am most anxious to stuff your dog there. At no charge, you understand," he added in a surprising display of generosity.

Mr. Schultz's face was now redder than ever and he, undoubtedly considering himself the innocent cause of all this trouble, also let loose with an outpouring of generosity. "No, no," he cried. "I will pay for stuffing the dog!"

The old man evidently heard all of this without understanding a word and he continued to shiver with fear.

"Look here, you must drink this glass of brandy," said Mueller at last, seeing that his mysterious visitor was intent upon getting away at all costs.

Mueller gave him the glass, which the old fellow took mechanically, but his hand trembled and before he had time to lift the brandy to his lips he had spilled more than half of it. He put the glass down again on the serving tray without having touched a drop. Then, with a strange laugh completely inappropriate under the circumstances, he unsteadily, but quickly, made his way out of the shop, leaving Azorka stretched out on the floor.

The others were astonished by this behavior and one of the Germans remarked, "Well, did you ever see the likes of that?"

"That's a nice sort of thing to happen!" remarked another German as they all stared blankly at each other.

As for me, I darted out in pursuit of the old man. A few paces from the shop there was a little street, narrow and dark, bordered by high houses, and I had a feeling that he must have turned in there. The second building on the right side of this street was a house in the process of construction, surrounded by scaffolding. This scaffolding stretched nearly into the middle of the road and I caught sight of the old man hiding in the shadows made by the scaffolding and the wall of the next house. He was sitting on the curb, his elbows resting on his knees, and he held his head between his two hands. I sat down by his side.

"Come, come," I said, having no idea how to begin. "You mustn't feel so miserable about poor Azorka. Let me take you home. Here, I'll hire a cab and we'll drive there together. Where do you live?"

He made no answer. I didn't know what to do. The street was empty. Suddenly he seized my hand.

"I'm choking! I'm choking!" he said. His voice was feeble and hoarse.

"Well, I'll take you home. Come," I said, lifting him by force. "You must have a cup of tea and get to bed. I'll call a cab. I'll get you a doctor, one of my friends."

I don't remember what else I said to him. He tried to get up, but when he was half on his feet he fell down again and began to mutter once more with that dreadful choking voice of his. I bent over him again and listened.

"Vasilyevsky." The word rattled in the old man's throat. "Sixth Line... Six... Sixth Line." He said no more, and was silent again.

"You live on Vasilyevsky Island, do you?" I asked. "But you were not going in that direction. You should have turned left and not right. You must go this way! Come with me, I'll take you there!"

He did not budge. I took his hand, but it fell back lifeless. I looked at his face, then touched it. He was dead. It seemed to me that all this was happening in a dream.

Well, this adventure caused me a great deal of worry and trouble, but as a result of it my feverish attack passed by itself. As others began to gather in the street, I was eventually able to learn where the old man lived. It was not on Vasilyevsky Island, but a step or two from the very spot where he had breathed his last, on the fifth floor of Klugen's house, just below the roof. He had a small hallway and a large room with a very low ceiling and three little skylights to serve for windows. The old fellow had existed there in great poverty. For furniture he had nothing but a table, two chairs and an old bed as hard as stone and with fibers of some coarse stuffing sticking out all over it. I discovered later that even this miserable furniture did not belong to him, but to the landlord. I could see that the stove had not been heated for ages and there was not a single candle to be found. Quite probably, his one reason for going to Mueller's was to sit in a warm room with light.

On the table there was an earthenware jug with nothing in it and an old crust of bread, as dry as a board. There was not a single kopek to be found and not even a change of linen to be buried in. Someone came forward and provided a shirt.

It was clear that he could not have lived like this, absolutely alone, so isolated. Somebody must have come by to look after him, however rarely. His passport was in the drawer of the table. The dead man had been a foreigner, but was a naturalized Russian subject. His name was Jeremiah Smith, his calling a mechanic, and his age 78. On the table were two books, an abridged geography and a New Testament in Russian, the margins of which were covered with pencil and fingernail marks. I took these two books for myself. I made inquiries of the other inhabitants of the house and of the landlord. They hardly knew anything about him. There were quite a few other lodgers in the house, mostly mechanics and German widows, who occupied furnished rooms with board and service. The landlord knew nothing of his late lodger other than that he used to pay six rubles per month for his room and that he had not settled for the last month, so the landlord had been obliged to give the old man notice to vacate.

I asked the neighbors whether anyone ever came to visit Mr. Smith, but nobody could give a satisfactory answer to my question. The house was a large one and so many people came in and out of the arched gateway that it was difficult to keep track of everyone. The porter who had manned the gate for the past five years could no doubt have given some information, but he had gone home to his village two weeks earlier and had left his nephew in charge, a young fellow who did not as yet know half the inhabitants of the house.

I'm not at all sure that my inquiries had helped in any way, but the old man was buried at last. In spite of all sorts of other business which I had on hand, I went over to Vasilyevsky Island every day, to the Sixth Line. I almost laughed at myself for doing so. What could I find in the Sixth Line but a row of houses? But then I thought, "Why did the old man talk about the Sixth Line at the very moment of his death? Or could he have been simply raving?"

As soon as his apartment was made available, I took it for myself. I liked it, especially the size of the room, although the ceiling was so low that at first I was afraid that I would bang my head, but I soon got used to it. In any event, one couldn't expect much better for six rubles a month, and I liked the absolute independence and isolation of the space. There was nothing to take care of now except to find someone to serve me, until which time the porter agreed to come in at least once a day to tidy up and to act as waiter on special occasions.

I hoped too that somebody would come and inquire about the old man, but he had been dead five days now and as yet no one had turned up.

Chapter Two

At this time, that is about a year ago, I was on the writing staff of several journals, contributing short articles to each, but I felt sure that I could develop into an author of more important works, and at the moment I was working on a novel. All of my many efforts ultimately led me to where I am today, stretched out in a hospital bed so sick that, as far as I can determine, I am on the straight road to death. But if the end is so near, why am I taking the time to write down these reminiscences?

No matter how I try to resist it, this last and most painful year of my life continues to invade my thoughts. I am going to write the whole thing down because I believe that unless I do so, I shall simply die of sorrow. All of these bitter memories torment me. At the point of my pen, perhaps they will settle down in an orderly fashion and appear much less like a ghastly dream or nightmare. Just the mechanical act of writing has a tranquilizing effect. It calms me and reawakens within me my old habits as a writer and transforms my nightmarish and delirious visions into palpable shape, into real work. Yes, this is a good idea! Now, if I die, at least my attendant shall inherit my memoirs. He can seal the double frames of his windows with my manuscript when winter comes.

I started my story in the middle, I don't know why. At any rate, I must write it all down, so let's begin again at the beginning. My autobiography shall, at least, not be a long one.

I was born, not in St. Petersburg, but a long way from this city. My parents were good enough people, I suppose, but they left me an orphan when I was very young and I grew up in the house of Nikolai Sergeich Ichmenyev, the landowner of a small estate who took me in out of pity. He had but one daughter, Natasha, three years younger than me, and she and I grew up together like brother and sister. Oh, what wonderful childhood days! What a tragic joke that all I have to look back on (and regret) at twenty-five years of age is you, Natasha. That at the hour of my death, you are all I can look back on with joy and love. The sun used to shine so brightly. It was so different from this St. Petersburg sun. Our young hearts used to beat so joyously then, when we were surrounded by green fields and woods and not by piles of inanimate stones. How marvelous were the park and garden at Vassilyevskoe, the property on which Nikolai Sergeich was steward. Natasha and I used to walk together in that garden and in the damp forest which stretched beyond it.

Such happy times. There, life first revealed its sweet mysteries to us as we explored them together. I used to think that some mysterious being, unknown and unfathomable, existed hidden beneath each tree, within each shrub. The world of fairy tales and the world of reality merged into one for us, and often when the mists of evening were thicker than usual over the dark valleys, Natasha and I would stand together, hand in hand, overlooking the whirlpool in the river, and would look in each other's faces in the darkness and wait, with a fearful curiosity, to see something stalking out of the mist, or to hear some voice speaking to us out of the depths of the canyon, and to find that our nurse's tales were about to prove to be pure truth.

Once, years later, I reminded Natasha of the day when they first gave us a book to read called *First Readings for Children*, and how we immediately ran off into the garden near the little pond where there was a grassy bank beneath an old maple, and how we settled down there and read Madame de Genlis' fairy story, *Alphonso and Dalinda*. To this moment, I cannot think of that tale without strange emotion, and only last year, when I repeated the first lines of it to Natasha ("Alphonso, the hero of my tale, was born in Portugal; Don Kamir, his father," etc.), the tears came to my eyes. I must have looked very foolish, for Natasha could not help smiling, which contrasted oddly with my serious demeanor. She saw my reaction, however, and to make amends she began to talk over the past with me, and while she spoke she too had been moved.

Oh, those delightful evenings we spent together, reminiscing over the past. And on the day I left for boarding school, how she cried, and again when we next parted, when I left Vassilyevskoe to continue my studies at the University. I was seventeen years old and she was going on fifteen. She has since told me that I was at that time a gawky, awkward boy, so badly put together that no one could look at me without laughing. When the moment came for parting, I remember that I took her aside to tell her something of terrific importance, but my tongue refused to utter a sound; it was paralyzed, and we had no conversation at all. I did not know what to say and I knew that she would not have understood what I meant. Anyhow, I wept hot tears over her and went away without having said a word. We did not see each other again until two years later, after her father had moved with his family to St. Petersburg as a result of the lawsuit, just as I was beginning my literary career.

CHAPTER THREE

Nikolai Sergeich Ichmenyev belonged to an honorable, but no longer wealthy, family. Upon the death of his parents, he had inherited a sizable piece of property, along with a hundred and fifty serfs. When he was twenty, he joined the hussars and had already served for six years (advancing to the rank of lieutenant) when one unfortunate evening he lost all of his property in a card game. He did not sleep a wink that night, but the next day reappeared at the card table and bet his horse, which was all he had left, on a single card. That card happened to win. So did the next one, and a third one, and in less than an hour he had won back fifty of his one hundred and fifty serfs along with the little estate known as Ichmenyevka.

He then gave up card playing, applied for his discharge from the army, received it two months later, and returned to vegetate on his property. He never again mentioned the circumstances just described and undoubtedly would have quarreled with anyone who dared to remind him of them.

He studied rural economy assiduously after that and a few years later, at the age of thirty-five, he married a young lady who came from a good, but poor, family named Anna Andreyevna Shoumiloff. Although she had no dowry and brought not a single kopek to the marriage, Anna Andreyevna prided herself on her proper education at a high-class school run by a French refugee named Madame Reveche, although no one could ever determine of what this magnificent education consisted.

Nikolai Sergeich developed into a first-rate scientific farmer and his neighbors looked upon him as a role model.

He lived in this quiet fashion for some years, until one eventful day when Prince Peter Alexandrovich Valkovsky (a neighboring landowner whose estate, Vassilyevskoe, boasted nine hundred serfs) arrived from St. Petersburg.

His arrival made a great sensation in the neighborhood. Although not quite in the first bloom of youth, the prince was still in the prime of life. His position was good, he had influential relatives, and he was handsome, rich and a widower. This last fact rendered him particularly attractive to all of the girls and young marriageable women in the neighborhood. People spoke of the brilliant reception which had been accorded him by the governor (who was discovered to be a distant relative of the prince). In short, he was one of those brilliant representatives of the highest St. Petersburg society, so rarely seen in the provinces, who produce such an extraordinary effect when they do make an appearance there.

However, it appeared that Prince Valkovsky was not quite as sweet as honey to *everyone*, especially not to those who could not benefit him in some way, his inferiors. Nor did he consider it useful to make the acquaintance of the other landowners near his own estate, which fact alone made him many enemies. What then must have been the general astonishment when he decided to pay a visit to Nikolai Sergeich? It was true, however, that the latter certainly was his nearest neighbor.

The arrival of the prince was a major event in the Ichmenyevs' home. From the very first day, Nikolai Sergeich and Anna Andreyevna were noticeably charmed by him, especially the latter whose enthusiasm knew no bounds. After a very short while, the prince felt perfectly at home with them, would visit almost every day, invited them to his home, cracked jokes with them, and sang and played on their wretched old piano. The Ichmenyevs could never see enough of him. How could anyone accuse so amiable, so agreeable a man of being proud and egotistical, as some of his neighbors insisted? Nikolai Sergeich, simple, honest, noble and disinterested fellow that he was, had certainly made a good impression on the prince, as was very soon made clear.

Valkovsky had come from St. Petersburg to dismiss his steward, a treacherous German with respectable white hair, a Roman nose and eyeglasses, who stole from his master shamelessly and who had been responsible for the death of several peasants whom he had cruelly mistreated. This miserable creature, caught in the act of pillaging the prince's finances, played the injured innocent and talked a great deal about German honestly, but Valkovsky fired him nonetheless.

The prince needed a new steward and his choice fell upon Nikolai Sergeich, who was certainly a perfect manager and honest in the full sense and meaning of the term. Valkovsky would have liked Ichmenyev to offer himself as the new steward, but when he failed to do so the prince decided one morning to make the proposal himself in the friendliest possible manner and in the form of a humble request. Nikolai Sergeich declined the offer, but the financial inducements (which were considerable) were most seductive to Anna Andreyevna, and the amiability of the prince become so pronounced that Nikolai Sergeich changed his mind and the prince at last achieved his goal.

It is clear that Valkovsky excelled in his understanding of human nature. The short space of time in which he had known the Ichmenyevs was quite enough for him to recognize that Nikolai Sergeich must be won over by friendship, by attachment of the heart, without which the temptation of money would mean very little to him. What the prince required was a steward in whom he could put his complete confidence so that he would never need to return to Vassilyevskoe unless he so desired. The charm which he exercised on Ichmenyev was so great that the latter sincerely believed that they were friends.

Nikolai Sergeich was one of those naïve, trusting and romantic individuals, so common in Russia, who easily attach themselves to others who are often quite unworthy of them, who give themselves heart and soul to their friends, and sometimes carry their devotion to a point which approaches the absurd.

Years passed. Valkovsky's lands were flourishing and he and his steward never had the slightest disagreement, their interaction exclusively confined to business correspondence. The prince, who never interfered in the slightest degree with any of his steward's arrangements, sometimes gave Nikolai Sergeich advice which astonished the latter by its practical and intelligent character. It was obvious that the prince not only disliked needless expenditure, but also understood the art of making a profit.

Five years after his visit to Vassilyevskoe, Valkovsky sent Ichmenyev orders for the purchase of another estate in the same neighborhood. It was a magnificent property of four hundred serfs. Nikolai Sergeich admired the prince tremendously and was so wholeheartedly interested in the prince's successes, in the attainment of his objects, in his advancement, that he worked as hard for the prince as he would have for his own brother.

But his enthusiasm reached its utmost limits when, as I am about to relate, the prince placed in his steward an amount of confidence which was really extraordinary.

However, as the prince is one of the chief actors in my story, I think I had better give a few details of his life prior to the events to be related.

CHAPTER FOUR

I have already said that Valkovsky was a widower. While still young he had married money. His family, who had always lived in Moscow, was quite ruined. His father had left him nothing but the estate at Vassilyevskoe, burdened with debt and a mortgage, so that at the age of twenty-two he had found himself penniless and forced to enter into government service in an office in Moscow, beginning his working life as the wretched sprout of an ancient but withered family tree. His marriage to the mature daughter of a merchant farmer saved him. Although her dowry was considerably less than he had been expecting, it was enough for the prince to clear his paternal acreage of debt and to plant his foot once again upon his own soil.

The merchant's daughter was quite unattractive, could barely write her own name, could not read two words in sequence, and had but one admirable quality: she had a sweet, good-natured personality. Valkovsky knew precisely how best to take advantage of this characteristic. After a year of marriage, he left his wife and a newborn son with her father in Moscow and went off to accept a prominent government post in another province, a position he had obtained through an influential relative in St. Petersburg. He thirsted for distinction and was determined to advance in his career. Knowing that he could not live with his wife in either St. Petersburg or Moscow, he resolved to begin his career in the provinces and wait for better times.

He treated his wife with the greatest cruelty. It was said that during their first year of married life he had very nearly killed her. (These reports would later arouse the greatest indignation in Nikolai Sergeich, who firmly sided with the prince and declared his master to be utterly incapable of any sort of vile behavior.)

After seven years of marriage, the prince became a widower and moved to St. Petersburg.

His arrival created quite a sensation in the capital. Still young, handsome, rich and with a great many shining virtues (including taste, geniality and unending good humor), he made his entrance into society not as a man seeking fortune and advancement but as one who projected a remarkable air of independence. He had, it was said, a sort of aura about him which commanded admiration and respect. Women adored him and a scandal concerning his involvement with a certain woman of the world only benefited his reputation further. He spent his money freely (although in private life he remained astonishingly frugal), and when he lost at cards he did so without betraying the slightest emotion no matter how large the sum lost.

One of his cousins, Count Nainsky, who would never have taken notice of the prince had he simply come forward as a vulgar fortune seeker, was delighted by his success in society. He thought it not only possible, but advantageous, to honor him with some attention, and he welcomed the prince's seven year old son, Alexey Petrovich Valkovsky, into his household to be educated.

It was just at this point in time that Valkovsky went to Vassilyevskoe and made himself known to the Ichmenyevs.

Through the influence of the count, the prince was appointed an attaché to one of the principal embassies and went abroad. There were countless tales (always cloaked in mystery and never naming names) that hinted at the prince's scandalous affairs and business dealings, but no one knew for sure exactly what the details were. All that was positively known was that the prince was suddenly able to afford to purchase an estate with more than four hundred serfs, the estate I mentioned earlier.

After several years, the prince (having attained a high rank in government service) returned to Russia and found an excellent appointment in St. Petersburg. Word soon reached Ichmenyevka that the prince was about to marry again into a rich and powerful family and Nikolai Sergeich was delighted.

I was in St. Petersburg at the time, studying at the University, and Nikolai Sergeich wrote to me inquiring about the rumors and wondering if the reports of the impending marriage were true. He also wrote a letter of recommendation to the prince concerning me, but never received an answer. For my part, all that I could determine was that Valkovsky's son had been educated in Count Nainsky's household, then at the Lyceum, and that at the age of nineteen he had completed his studies. I gave Ichmenyev these fragments of information and added that the prince was very fond of his son, spoiled him, and had already made plans for his future, all of which I learned from several other students at the University who knew the young prince.

Shortly after that, Ichmenyev received a letter from Valkovsky which greatly surprised him. Until that moment the prince had restricted his correspondence with his steward to formal business matters, but suddenly he wrote Ichmenyev a frank, cordial letter about his family affairs. He complained about his son, Alexey Petrovich, whose conduct was causing him a great deal of distress. While he did not want to attach more significance to his son's rebellious behavior than the usual indiscretions of youth (he evidently wanted to downplay the nature of his son's offenses), he had resolved to punish the boy and to frighten him, and therefore wished to send him to live in the country with the Ichmenyevs, who would act as his guardians. The prince put himself entirely in the hands of his "honorable and excellent friend," and of his wife, and begged them to take the foolish, wayward youth into their family; to make him listen to the voice of reason while in exile; to love him, if possible, but most importantly to instill in the boy an understanding of the "moral and ethical behavior necessary to succeed in life."

The young prince arrived and was welcomed into the family like a son. Nikolai Sergeich soon loved him as he did his daughter, Natasha, and sometime later when he quarreled with the boy's father, he often thought with joy of his dear Alyosha (as he used to call the young prince, Alexey Petrovich).

He was certainly a charming young man, as pretty and as delicate as a girl, cheerful and trusting, with a heart endowed with sincerity and an openness to the noblest sentiments, an affectionate personality, honest and sympathetic. He soon became the idol of the Ichmenyev family.

He was, in spite of his twenty years, still a child, and it was difficult to understand why his father, who was supposedly so fond of him, had sent him into exile. He had led, it was rumored, a troublesome, unruly life in St. Petersburg, and had refused to enter into government service, which had annoyed his father. Ichmenyev never asked any questions, because he gathered from Valkovsky's letter that he wished to say nothing about the real reasons for his son's exile. According to one rumor, the boy had been guilty of unpardonable wildness. Another talked of a love affair, another of a duel, and still another of huge gambling debts. But there were some people who attributed the prince's action to certain personal considerations of a secret nature, to a calculating and egotistical scheme of the prince's own.

Ichmenyev repudiated all of these rumors with indignation, especially as the young man was greatly attached to his father, whom he had hardly known during his childhood and youth, but of whom he never spoke except with enthusiasm, and whom he evidently regarded with unquestionable allegiance.

Occasionally, Prince Alexey spoke of some countess and of a rivalry between his father and himself. It appeared that he had come between his father and the countess which made his father furious. Alexey used to tell this story with great animation and a sort of childish glee, but Ichmenyev refused to listen and stopped the boy whenever he attempted to tell it. Alexey did confirm, however, the rumors that the prince had matrimonial plans for him.

He had now spent a year in exile, and wrote occasionally to his father, most respectful and reasonable letters. By this time, Alexey had grown so used to living at Ichmenyevka that when his father came down in the spring on business, Alexey begged his father to be allowed to stay on as long as possible, assuring his father that he felt a real affinity for country-life. Every action, every impulse of Alexey's proceeded from his excessive impressionability and nervousness, from his warmth of heart, from his extraordinary readiness to succumb to any exterior influence, and from his almost absurd inability to take any action or think any thought of his own.

The prince received his son's request with a considerable show of opposition. Ichmenyev had some difficulty in recognizing his old friend, who had completely changed. The prince had become mean and petty, and in examining financial matters had showed himself to be repugnant and disagreeably combative. This was a source of great sorrow to Ichmenyev, who could not acknowledge it at first. However, everything was exactly the opposite of what had happened during the prince's previous visit, fourteen years earlier. This time, the prince made the acquaintance of all of the surrounding neighbors (the most important ones, that is), but never set foot in the Ichmenyevs' home, treating them as inferiors.

One day, something inconceivable happened. Without any apparent cause, there was a stormy argument between Valkovsky and Ichmenyev during which violent words were exchanged, offensive epithets were tossed, and Ichmenyev left the house indignant and angry. But that was not the end of it. Odious stories began to circulate in the district that Ichmenyev had been studying the character of the young prince in order to take advantage of the boy's weaknesses; that his daughter, Natasha, had manipulated her way into the boy's heart; and that, while pretending to notice nothing of it, Ichmenyev and his wife had encouraged their artful and depraved daughter to bewitch the innocent young man. As a result of such cunning, during the entire year he had spent with the Ichmenyevs, Alexey had never even set eyes on any of the other young girls in the neighborhood, whose beauty and charms were ripening within the family seats of the neighboring gentry. People went so far as to suggest that the young couple had arranged to elope to the neighboring village of Grigorievo, all with the consent and active participation of the girl's scheming parents. In short, a thick book would not hold the volume of wretched gossip which the scandal-mongers of the neighborhood, both men and women, succeeded in circulating.

What was most astonishing of all is that the prince believed every word of it. In fact, he had only come down to Vassilyevskoe in response to an anonymous letter sent to him in St. Petersburg. It would certainly seem that anyone with even the slightest knowledge of Ichmenyev's character would have refused to believe a word of all this, and yet, as often happens in such cases, everyone preoccupied themselves with the rumors, talked about them, blamed Ichmenyev, shook their heads, and passed judgment without question.

Ichmenyev had too much pride to justify his daughter to a troop of gossipers, and he solemnly forbade his wife to enter into any kind of explanation on the subject with her neighbors. Natasha, so cruelly maligned for the better part of a year, never heard a word of any of these trumped-up lies and continued to be as happy and innocent as a child.

Meanwhile, the quarrel grew more and more venomous. The gossipers and scandal-mongers were relentless and witnesses turned up to denounce Ichmenyev, never failing to convince the prince that Ichmenyev's handling of his estate's affairs had been less than honest. They went so far as to "prove" that three years earlier, during the sale of a forest, Ichmenyev had embezzled twelve thousand rubles from the proceeds, an action made all the more suspicious because the prince had not requested that the timber be sold, but had been convinced by Ichmenyev of the necessity for the sale and, after it was all over, had received from his steward considerably less than had actually been received.

These were all pure fabrications, as was proven later, but the prince believed them at the time and in the presence of witnesses accused Ichmenyev of theft. The latter could not bear the affront and responded to the prince with equal fervor. A dreadful quarrel followed and a lawsuit was started.

Ichmenyev soon saw that his case would fail. He required certain papers and, above all, he needed guidance and advice. He had absolutely no experience in such matters and it looked like he would lose the case and have his property confiscated. The indignant old man determined to move his home to the capital in order to look after his legal interests in connection with the lawsuit. He left an agent in whom he had complete confidence in charge of Ichmenyevka and set off for St. Petersburg.

Valkovsky, more than likely, soon realized that he had unjustly defamed Ichmenyev, but the insults had flown so freely from both sides that it was now impossible to find a means of reconciliation, and the angry prince did all he could to turn the situation to his own profit, which simply meant taking the last bit of bread out of his old steward's mouth.

CHAPTER FIVE

So the Ichmenyevs moved to St. Petersburg. I will not describe my meeting with Natasha, who during the four years of our separation had never for a moment been out of my thoughts, but I will confess that my first thought upon seeing her again was that Fate had finally awarded her to me. It seemed to me at first that she had not matured much, that she had remained very much the girl-child of the days before our separation, but as time went on, I began to see new wonders in her every day, things which I had not seen before, perhaps because she had concealed them from me on purpose, as if the girl had wanted to hide her perfections from my eyes. And, oh, the joy of those discoveries!

During the period of his stay in St. Petersburg, Nikolai Sergeich was peevish and irritable. His affairs were not going well. He used to get angry and bury himself in his papers and take no notice of us. Anna Andreyevna, his wife, was like one lost and did not know what to do with herself. St. Petersburg terrified her and she would sigh and tremble and lament about the old haunts where she had passed her life up till then. She would complain that Natasha had arrived at a marriageable age and there was nobody who gave her a second thought. She began to confide her deepest feelings in me, probably because there was no one else around better qualified to receive her confidences.

I had just finished my first novel and as a beginner I did not know the first thing about getting it published. I decided not to tell the Ichmenyevs anything about it until it was sold, and they were nearly ready to quarrel with me for leading a life of indolence, without employment and without making any effort to find employment. My adopted father criticized me severely and, as I knew his arguments were prompted by his paternal affection for me, I felt ashamed of telling him how I actually spent my time. How could I, in good conscience, tell him straight out that I did not want to be a "functionary," and that my function was to write novels? Instead I told him that I had not yet found a job, but that I was doing all that I could to find one. He, however, had no time to bother about my affairs just then.

Natasha had been present during one of my conversations with her father and later took me aside and implored me, with tears in her eyes, to think of my future. She questioned me about how I spent my time, but I didn't tell her my secret either, so she made me swear not to make myself wretched by my sloth and idleness. I just couldn't tell her about my novel yet, even though I am quite sure that one word of encouragement from her would have given me far more joy than all the flattering judgments which I later received.

My novel appeared at last, but long before its publication it was talked about in the literary world and Belinsky, himself, had rejoiced like a child over my manuscript.

If ever I was happy, it was not during those first intoxicating moments of my success, but rather during that period when I had not yet read or shown my work to a single soul. It was during those long nights of dreaming and of hopeful anticipation, while I labored passionately and lived among the characters that I had created, as though they were family members, living and breathing and real. I loved them and shared their joys and sorrows. Indeed, I remember now and again being actually moved to tears by the stupidity of one of my heroes.

I cannot describe the joy felt by my adopted parents, the Ichmenyevs, when they first heard the whisper of my success. Their first sensation was stunned silence. Anna Andreyevna simply would not believe that this new writer whom all the world was praising was her very own Vanya, and she simply shook her head in wonder.

The old man took even longer to acknowledge the situation after he first heard the news. He was deeply concerned and warned me that I would lose all hope of making a career in government service and spoke to me of the uncertain life led by most authors. However, the favorable notices which appeared in the newspapers and a few words of praise on my behalf from men he respected soon changed his opinion. As soon as he saw that I had money too and understood how well literary work can be remunerated, his last scruples vanished. Quick to leap from doubt to absolute confidence, as happy as a child for my success, he abandoned himself all at once to the most foolish aspirations on my account, to daydreams of the most dazzling description as to my future. Every day he invented some new career for me or planned some new project. He even began to assume towards me a deferential demeanor which he had certainly never demonstrated before. Every once in a while his doubts would return and interrupt him even in the midst of one of his most exuberant fantasies, baffling and confusing him. To be an author! A poet! What a foolish occupation! What poet ever made his way in the world or attained greatness? There was nothing to be made of all these scribblers; worthless crew, the whole lot of them!

These doubts and confusions generally assailed him at the twilight hour. It was during that period of the day especially when he was most impressionable, nervous and suspicious. Natasha and I recognized this and generally found his behavior amusing. I would try to make him take a less pessimistic view of the matter by telling him amusing stories about General Soumorokof, or about how Derjavine sent snuff boxes filled with gold pieces, or how the Empress Catherine had personally visited the University. I spoke of Pushkin and of Gogol.

"I know, my friend, I know all that," he would say, though likely enough he had never heard a word of these stories until then. "I know all that, but what comforts me a little in your case is that your cooking is not stewed in verse. Poetry, my dear boy, is simply absurd. Now, don't argue with me. Take this from an old man who wishes you well. Poetry is a waste of time. It's one thing for college professors to go in for rhyming, but for a young fellow of your age, my boy, it's the straight road to the lunatic asylum. Pushkin is a great man, no one can deny him that, but verses and nothing but verses, simply nonsense. Not that I've read much poetry, but prose, now that is another thing altogether. An author can instruct, can talk of patriotism and virtue. I'm not a good hand at explaining things, but you know what I mean. It's my love for you that makes me speak to you like this. But let's have a look at what you're going to read to us," he concluded in a patronizing tone on the day I at last brought them a copy of my book. We were all sitting together around the table after tea.

"Now then," he added, "read us a bit of what you've been scribbling all this time. You have managed to get yourself talked about a good deal, let's see what's in it!"

The novel had appeared that very day and as soon as I could get my hands on a copy I ran with it to the Ichmenyevs. I was unhappy that I couldn't read it to them earlier, but the manuscript had been in the publisher's hands. Natasha scolded me about my allowing strangers to read my novel before her.

The family assembled, I opened my book to read. Nikolai Sergeich assumed an air of the utmost solemnity for he was prepared to bring the most severe criticism to bear upon my work. He wanted to form his own opinion and to convince himself as to its merits. Anna Andreyevna also assumed a far more serious air than she normally wore. She even put on a new bonnet expressly in honor of the reading. For a long time she had been aware that I regarded her Natasha with infinite love, that my spirit was nourished on her image and that my eyes darkened when I spoke to her. Natasha's eyes too looked at me more brightly than before. The time was near, I felt, when success would finally fulfill my golden dreams and bring me the happiness I longed for.

Natasha's mother had also observed the tendency on her husband's part to praise me extravagantly and to look at me and his daughter with a new and peculiar expression on his face, and she suddenly took fright. I was not a count or a prince or a reigning duke. If only I were some fine young fellow just out of law school, full of wisdom and honors! But what is a writer?

CHAPTER SIX

I read them the whole novel in one sitting, beginning after tea and not finishing until two in the morning. Nikolai Sergeich, at first, frowned. He had envisioned something on some inexplicably higher level, something that he might not be able to understand, but that would be important. Instead, what he had heard seemed so commonplace, the events were no different from his own daily experiences, the characters just like people he met every day. He had been anticipating some lofty hero performing great deeds or, at the very least, some historical figure like Pushkin's Roslavlev or Zagoskin's Yuri Miloslavsky. But instead he had been presented with a common little clerk, obscure, foolish and so poor that his shabby coat was missing its buttons, and the language had been so simple, so straightforward, so much like ordinary conversation, that he had understood every word of it. It was most surprising to him, and I think he felt that he had been deprived of something special. Anna Andreyevna exchanged glances with her husband and with a shrug seemed to be saying, "Will people really pay money to read about such depressing, commonplace people?"

Natasha, however, had listened with rapt attention, holding my hand in hers, never taking her eyes off me, and seemed almost to be reading along with me as she watched my lips move. I had read little more than half of my novel when I noticed all three of them crying. Anna Andreyevna had been sincerely moved by my hero's plight and her tears and exclamations seemed to suggest that she would have gladly helped him if she could, anything to relieve his misery.

The old man, after a few moments, set aside his higher aspirations. "From the very beginning," he said, "it is evident that it is going to be a long journey from first to last, but it is a simple tale that seizes the heart. The actions that occur are understandable and it is quite memorable, really. It seems to be saying that even the most oppressed person on earth is also a man and deserves to be called my brother."

Natasha suddenly rose, her cheeks and eyes red with tears. She grasped my hand quickly, kissed it, and ran out of the room. Her father and mother exchanged surprised glances.

"Well," said the old man, trying to justify his daughter's odd behavior to both me and himself. "That is good! She has been moved by your story. It was a fine noble impulse! She is a good girl, Natasha, a very good girl." But Anna Andreyevna, despite having been clearly moved during the reading, looked upon me now in a disapproving manner, as if to say, "It may be true that your character, Alexander Makedonsky is a hero in his own way, but why does he have to break the chairs?"

Natasha soon returned, looking radiant and happy once again, and pinched me as she passed by me.

The old man returned once again to his critique of my novel, speaking at first in a very "serious" tone of voice, but soon revealing his enthusiasm. "Well, Vanya, it is good, quite good! Comforting. Not high art, not great, of course, that is clear. Not like Dmitriyev's *The Liberation of Moscow*, in which the spirit of man seems to soar like an eagle, but in its own way it seems, from the very first line, to speak for all men, so to speak. You understand, Vanya, that in your own simple language you have made it most intelligible. Yes, precisely that! I love that it is intelligible! The people seem to talk like me, the events are so much like my own life. Not high art, perhaps, but a simple style, easily understood. You have done very well, indeed, Vanya. And what else is there to say? It is printed, it is too late to change anything. Perhaps in the second edition? Ah, will you be paid again for a second edition?"

"Yes, they pay well for this sort of thing, do they?" asked Anna Andreyevna. "The more I think about it, the more unbelievable it all seems. My lord, the things that people will spend their money on."

"You know, Vanya," the old man continued, growing more intrigued by the subject, "this occupation of writing may not be on the same level as government service, but there is still something honorable in it. Even high ranking people will read your book and you have mentioned, I think, that Gogol receives a yearly pension and lives comfortably abroad. And that may happen to you! But, of course, it is too soon to talk about such things. You need to write more books, even better books. So write, brother, write faster, you mustn't rest on your laurels! Strike while the iron is hot!"

He spoke with such conviction and with such warmth of heart that I did not want to stop him or to do anything to stifle his enthusiasm.

"They may even give you a snuff-box," he added. "Why not? They will want to encourage you. And, who knows, you may even be invited to court." He said this in a whisper, with a wink of his eye. "Or, perhaps, it is too soon to talk about being invited to court."

"And why shouldn't he be invited to court?" said the mother, a little offended.

"You're going to make me a general before I know it," I laughed heartily. The old man laughed too, feeling very happy now.

"Come, Your Excellency, don't you want to eat something?" said Natasha, who had prepared a late supper for us. She was laughing and bouncing around as friskily as a puppy and ran to her father and threw herself into his arms. "My darling, darling, papa!" She was overcome with emotion and her father was too.

"Yes, yes, my sweet daughter, it is all very funny, but general or no general, it's time for supper. You are such a sweet, sensitive child," he said, patting her cheeks with his large hands. "You know, Vanya, you may not be a general, oh no, far from a general, but you shall be someone important nonetheless. An author!"

"People call them writers nowadays, papa, not authors," Natasha said.

"Writers, not authors? I didn't know that. But what I was about to say, Vanya, is that you may not be appointed chamberlain, but you are now someone of importance. You may be sent abroad to Italy as an attaché or for your health or to study your art. You may even be provided with a subsidy while you write more books. The money would be wonderful, of course, but your honor depends on your earning such money and not in simply accepting the patronage of others."

"And you mustn't get a swollen head, either, Ivan Petrovich," added Anna Andreyevna with a laugh.

"Yes, but let him have at least a small medal to wear on his chest, papa. He deserves so much more than to be just an attaché." Natasha again laughed and pinched me on the hand.

"Ah, there she goes making fun of me," cried the old man with delight. Natasha's eyes flashed merrily and shone like stars in the candlelight. "I may have gone a little too far, but it seems to me, Vanya, when I look at you and compare you to many of the great writers, you seem so simple."

"Oh my God, papa, what do you expect him to look like?"

"No, no, I didn't mean it like that. Maybe I phrased it wrong, Vanya, but when I look at your face, it is not... well, poetic. You know, they speak of poets as pale, with their hair such and in their eyes there is such and, well, when I look at you I do not see the face of a poet. You're not Goethe, for example. Of course, that is not a bad thing. But look, my friend, I am not a philosopher or a scientist. I only know what I feel. So if your face is not the face of a poet, so be it, but I must add that it pleases me very much that there is no great misfortune in your face, yours is a good face, indeed. But you must remain honest, Vanya, be an honest man, that is the main thing. Live honestly and the road is wide open before you! That is what I wanted to say, precisely what I wanted to say!"

What a marvelous evening that was. There were many more fine evenings I spent with the Ichmenyevs. Frequently, I would bring news of the literary world, a subject in which the old man had suddenly taken considerable interest. He even began to read critical essays and scholarly articles in journals which he praised enthusiastically, even though he barely understood a word, and he could pontificate for hours on writers, both good and bad.

The old woman kept a vigilant watch over Natasha and me, but we managed to elude her on occasion. Fortunately, she didn't follow us about the house! Natasha and I needed very few words to communicate for we both understood each other completely. The one word I had longed to hear for so long finally came late one afternoon when Natasha, after casting her eyes down and turning her head away from me, whispered, "Yes."

Our love for each was no secret to her parents, but they remained somewhat skeptical about my chosen profession. "Indeed, you have had a great success with your first book, Ivan Petrovich," Anna Andreyevna told me one day, "but what will you do if the next one is not so well received? You may not always be so successful, and what then? At least if you had some steady employment..."

"This is what I have to say to you, Vanya," added the old man after thinking it over for a moment. "I have seen, noticed and recognized that there is something very special between you and Natasha, and it gladdens my heart even as it gladdens your own. Yes, that is all very well. But you see, Vanya, the two of you are still very young, and Anna Andreyevna and I are agreed that it is best for you both to wait. You have, of course, talent, Vanya, perhaps even remarkable talent, and it will no doubt take you far in the world. It may not be genius, as they first shouted about you—I read, in fact, today a criticism of your work in the newspaper—so let us say, simply, talent. But talent cannot be taken to the pawnshop and exchanged for money. You are both poor. Let us wait then for a year or, at the very least, half a year. By then you should be well along in your career and, if so, Natasha will be yours. But if you do not succeed, well then, you shall judge for yourself what is best. You are an honest man, I think." He stopped at this.

So we waited a year. In fact, it was almost exactly one year later when, on a clear September evening, I went to visit the Ichmenyevs with a great sadness in my heart. I was very ill and as I entered their home I almost fainted, falling into a chair, which alarmed them greatly. But if my head was dizzy and if my heart was palpitating, it was not because I had on ten recent occasions arrived at their door and then turned and gone back home again without entering, nor was it because I had so far failed to achieve any noticeable success as a writer (having earned neither fame nor financial reward), nor was it because I had not been appointed attaché to any government office, nor was it because I had not been sent by a grateful nation to Italy to recover my health. No. It was because I had come to recognize in the past year that two people, both Natasha and I, could live ten years in the space of just twelve months and that now an even greater abyss lay between us.

And here I sat before the old man and his wife. He settled silently into his chair, barely looking at me in my shabby suit which hung badly on my shrunken frame. My face too had grown thin and pale, though still not, I am sure, the old man's image of a poet. The old woman stared with undisguised pity at me, a look which saddened me for it seemed to say, "My lord, is this the man to whom we almost gave our Natasha?"

"Take a cup of tea, Ivan Petrovich," she said, pointing to the samovar on the table. "How are you feeling? Are you still under the weather?" The sadness in her voice still haunts me to this day. She turned her glance to her husband. It was clear that he too had been sick. The strain of the lawsuit had had a devastating effect on his health and he sat motionless, staring into space, a cup of tea sitting next to him cold and undisturbed.

The young prince, who had been the primary cause of the quarrel between his father and Ichmenyev, had started to visit the Ichmenyevs in their home some five months earlier. The old man, who loved Alexey like a son and mentioned him in conversation almost daily, was delighted by the visits. His wife said it reminded her of their years at Vassilyevskoe and tears came to her eyes. The young prince's visits soon grew more and more frequent and Ichmenyev, who personifies the virtues of honesty and openness, refused to take any precautionary measures. His pride kept him from accepting the idea that Valkovsky might respond negatively upon hearing of his son's repeated visits to their home, and, as a consequence, Alexey was soon visiting the family on a daily basis, often staying past midnight.

Word quickly reached Valkovsky, of course, and the resulting scandal gave rise to even worse gossip and scandal mongering than Ichmenyev had endured at Vassilyevskoe. The old prince sent Nikolai Sergeich an insulting letter and positively forbade his son to go near the Ichmenyevs. This had occurred just two weeks before my visit.

The old man was in a terrible state of depression. His sweet, innocent Natasha had once again become the object of distorted lies and outrageous accusations and he knew that the man responsible was the same villain who had slandered his own name so grossly, and there was little he could do to demand satisfaction.

The first few days were especially hard on him and he took to his bed in despair. I was able to keep up with the details of what transpired from my own sickbed at home and had not been near the Ichmenyevs for three weeks. During that time I had had a presentiment of still worse things to come and dared not allow my thoughts to dwell upon them. It was anguish for me to sit there now before my friends, trying to avoid thinking about the impending storm, and knowing that there was nothing I could do to avoid the inevitable.

As difficult as it was for me to face the family, I knew that I had to be there for Natasha's sake. There was something that drew me to her side this particular evening.

"Well," said the old man, shaking himself awake from his stupor. "Have you been sick or what? We haven't seen you in weeks. I know it's my fault, I should have come to see you, but there always seemed to be something that prevented it." Again he returned to his private thoughts.

"I'm afraid I've been rather grubby lately," I said.

He didn't respond for nearly five minutes, then finally said, "Ha! Grubby! Grubby. I've often told you to take better care of yourself, but you never listened. I suppose it is still necessary for artists to starve in garrets before the muse of inspiration will deign to visit them."

I knew that the old man must have been greatly distressed for him to talk to me like that, so I let it pass. I just looked at him. His face was yellow and his sad eyes had a puzzled look that seemed to ask a question that he was too tired or too confused to answer. He was more irritable than I had ever seen him.

His wife looked at him anxiously. When he wasn't looking she took the opportunity to give me a glance that clearly told me that she was worried about him.

"How has Natasha been feeling," I asked her. "Is she at home?"

"Yes, she's home," she answered, looking surprisingly embarrassed by her response. "I'm sure she will be out to see you soon. It is no joke when I tell you that she has changed greatly in the three weeks since you last saw each other, and we can't understand it. I don't know whether she is sick or what. God help her," she added, looking at her husband.

"No, no, she's fine, there's nothing at all wrong with her," Ichmenyev responded angrily, "she's not sick. She's just growing up. All girls are like that at her age. Who can understand a young woman's sorrows and whims?"

"Whims," said the mother. "You call them whims?"

The old man did not respond, but sat and drummed his fingers on the table. "My God," I thought to myself, "what has happened between these two to bring them to this state of affairs?"

"So, tell me, Vanya, what has been happening with you?" the old man asked again. "What is Belinsky doing? Does he still write criticisms?"

"Yes," I said, "he still writes."

The old man sat quietly for a moment, "Ah, Vanya," he said, waving his hand in a sad gesture of defeat, "there is already so much criticism."

Suddenly, the door opened and Natasha entered.

CHAPTER SEVEN

Natasha was carrying her hat in her hand as she entered, moved to set it down on the piano, then came to me and held out her hand without a word. Her lips moved slightly as if she wanted to say something to me, some friendly greeting perhaps, but no words came. We had not seen each other for three weeks and I was astonished by the change that had taken place in her. Her cheeks were pale and hollow, her lips parched with fever, but behind her dark eyelashes there was a fiery look of passionate determination. My God, she was beautiful. I could not remember her ever having looked more breathtaking than on that fateful day.

Was this the same Natasha who just one year earlier had trembled in sympathy with me as I read my novel, who had laughed so gaily and chided her father so affectionately during supper? The same Natasha who, there, in the next room, had turned her head, lowered her eyes, and told me "yes?"

Suddenly, a nearby church bell sounded its call to Vespers. Natasha trembled and Anna Andreyevna crossed herself.

"You should go to Vespers, Natasha, I know you want to. Go and pray. It's not far, and the walk will do you good. You don't get out enough and you always look so pale. It's as if someone has cast a spell over you."

"I don't think I will go today," she replied slowly in a voice so quiet and hoarse that I could scarcely hear her. "I don't feel well." The blood drained from her face.

"Why don't you go, my darling? You were on your way a moment ago. You've even brought your hat with you. Go. Go and pray to God to give you back your health."

"Yes, yes, your mother's quite right," said the old man. "You should go. You'll get a little fresh air at the same time. Vanya will walk with you."

I thought I saw a bitter smile on Natasha's lips. Her hand was trembling as she picked up her hat and put it on. Her movements seemed oddly mechanical, as if some unconscious force were compelling her against her will. Her father and mother watched her with astonishment.

"Good-bye," she said, in a scarcely audible voice.

"Why good-bye, my darling?" asked the mother. "You won't be gone long. It's just a short walk, you'll get a little air, and that will do you good. Oh lord, I had forgotten something important—I'm always so forgetful. I've made a little case for you. A man in Kiev taught me how to do it last year. It's a lovely little case and I've stitched a prayer inside it. It's a very appropriate prayer, my angel. Take it with you and, perhaps, the good Lord will send you back your health. You are our only child," and she took from her workbox a small golden cross which Natasha often wore around her neck. Anna Andreyevna had attached the little case to the same piece of ribbon that held the cross.

"Wear it in good health," she said, as she put the ribbon around Natasha's neck and made the sign of the cross. "There was a time when I used to baptize you like this every evening," she sobbed. "I used to read you a prayer before you went to sleep and you would repeat it back to me. But things are not the same now, my darling. You no longer feel the same tranquil spirit of the Lord. Oh, Natasha, Natasha! All I can give you is a mother's prayers and they don't seem to help you, they don't do you any good!" and she cried bitterly.

Natasha silently kissed her mother's hand and started in the direction of the door, but turned suddenly and went to her father, falling on her knees in front of him.

"Father, you must bless me too. Bless your daughter," she cried in a breathless voice.

We all exchanged confused glances as we stood and watched this solemn act. After a few moments, the old man looked down at her, completely bewildered.

"Natasha, my darling, my little one, my own dear little daughter, what is the matter with you?" he cried at last and a lifetime of tears ran down his cheeks. "Tell me why you are so sad? Why do you cry day and night? I see it all, you know. I don't sleep at night any better than you do, and I hear you crying. Tell me, my Natasha, open your heart to me and let your father share your troubles and we..." He did not finish, but lifted her into his arms and held her close. She pressed herself convulsively to her father's breast and buried her head in his shoulder.

"Nothing, it's nothing, I'm a bit under the weather, that's all," she said, her voice suffocated by a flood of tears that she could not suppress.

"May God bless you, even as I give you my blessing now, my darling, my precious child," said her father, "and may He send you peace from this time forward, and keep you from all harm! Pray to God, my darling, that my prayers may reach Him."

"And my blessing upon you too," added her mother, weeping.

"Good-bye," Natasha whispered.

As she reached the door, she stopped and looked once again at her parents as if she had something more to say, but couldn't, and ran quickly from the room. I rushed after her, with a presentiment of evil gaining strength within me.

CHAPTER EIGHT

Natasha was silent as we walked through the streets toward the River Neva. Her head was bowed low and she didn't look at me, but when we reached the embankment of the river she stopped suddenly and grabbed me by the hand.

"I'm suffocating," she said, "suffocating."

"Come back, Natasha," I cried in fright, "come back home."

"Don't you see, Vanya, that I've left them and that I can't ever return?" she said with the most sorrowful look imaginable.

My heart stopped. I had suspected that something like this would happen and yet her words struck me like a thunderbolt. As we walked along the embankment, I tried to think of something to say, but I felt entirely lost. My head was spinning. It all seemed so grotesque, so impossible!

"You blame me, Vanya," she said finally.

"No, but... I can't believe it, this just can't be!" I answered, not knowing what I was saying.

"And yet it's all true," she said. "I'm leaving and I don't know what will happen to them. I'm not even sure what will happen to me."

"You are going to him, aren't you?"

"Yes."

"But this is impossible, Natasha," I cried out angrily. "You know it's impossible! Oh, my poor Natasha, this is madness! It will kill *them* and destroy *you*. You know that, don't you?"

"Yes, I know it," she said, "but what can I do? I have no choice." I heard so much despair in her voice, it was as though she were about to climb the stairs of the scaffold to be hanged.

"Come back, Natasha, come back before it's too late!" I begged with all the passion I could muster, knowing the futility of my efforts and recognizing how utterly absurd this moment was. "Have you thought about what this will do to your father?" I fought with the only weapon I had available to me. "You know that your father and his father are bitter enemies because of the lies the prince told.

He humiliated and degraded your father by accusing him of embezzlement, by calling your father a thief! You know that he is suing your father in a court of law at this very moment and that he... my God, you must know this, Natasha... that he has accused your parents of encouraging you to seduce Alexey while he was with you in the country! Remember how your poor father has suffered from these insults, his hair has turned white! I won't say a word of what it will cost them to lose you, their one treasure, you, who are all that remains to them in their old age. You know all that already, but think about this, Natasha. Your father believes you to be as innocent as a lamb, that all the malicious stories about you and Alexey are simply lies. But now this has all flared up again and the prince has again insulted your father. Understand, Natasha, that if you do this, if you go to Alexey, suddenly all of the prince's vile accusations about you will be proven true, will be justified by your conduct. Everyone who has heard the insinuations and accusations against you and your father will now be able to say that the prince was right all along. The humiliation will kill your father, Natasha, the degradation, the shame of it all will kill him, and you will be responsible! You, Natasha, his innocent-as-a-lamb, little darling daughter. And your mother, do you think she will survive the old man's death? Natasha, please, think of what you are doing and wake up. Wake to your own self again, Natasha, and come home!"

She was silent, but the look in her eyes was filled with so much pain, such intense sorrow, that I realized how difficult her decision had been, and I knew that my cruel words were only torturing her more. I wanted to stop, but I felt compelled to continue.

"A little while ago you told your mother that you didn't want to go out, to go to Vespers. I think, at that moment, you were undecided about leaving home. Maybe you still have doubts."

She smiled bitterly. I knew that nothing I could say would change her mind, that it was useless to try.

"Do you really love him that much?" I asked, with a sinking feeling in my heart. I didn't know what else to say.

"How should I answer you, Vanya?" she finally responded. "It's simple. He told me to meet him here. I have done as he asked. I am here, waiting for him."

"But listen, listen," I begged, clutching at straws that were beyond my reach. "You can still do this, but there are other ways, better ways, to deal with this. You don't have to leave home. I'll help you to make other arrangements. I'll carry letters for you, help you to meet him in private, anything to make this easier than simply leaving home. Natasha, my love, you know that I will do anything to keep you from destroying your life. Meet with him in secret for just a little while, at least until your fathers end this stupid quarrel. Then, when the fighting is over, you and he will be free to love each other any way you please. You'll be very happy, really you will, Natasha, you'll see, and you won't have to give up everything!"

"Vanya, please stop!" she interrupted, grabbing my hand and smiling through her tears. "My dear, dear, Vanya, what a loyal and honest friend you are. You haven't said one word about yourself. I've walked out on you too and yet you forgive me, you think only about my happiness. Would you really carry letters for us?" she said with wonder and cried even harder. "I know how much you have loved me, Vanya, and how much you love me even now. And yet you have never uttered a single reproachful word, not one bitter thought. My God, I am the one to blame for all this. You remember every beautiful moment we have ever spent together. It would have been so much easier if I had never known, never even met him! You and I could have been so happy together. But I am not worthy of you. Why do you continue to talk about past happiness, what good does it do you? For three weeks I didn't see you, and I swear to you that not once in all that time did I think that you hated me or cursed me. I knew that you didn't want to come between us or to reproach us for our love. You refused to be an obstacle to my possible happiness. It must have been so painful for you to see us, and yet I did so long to see you. I love Alyosha madly, even more than madly, and yet sometimes it seems to me that I love you still more, but as my friend. I could never live without you. You are essential to me, my Vanya, you and your heart of gold! Oh, Vanya, what a bitter, terrible future we have!"

And her tears continued to flow. Yes, it was hard for me to watch.

"Oh, how I wanted to see you," she continued, trying to hold back her tears. "You look so thin and pale, have you been sick, Vanya? I didn't even ask about you. I talked only of myself! How are you doing now, Vanya? How is your novel going?"

"To hell with my novel, Natasha! Tell me, did Alexey insist on your eloping with him?"

"No, it was more my idea. Of course, he did say yes, and I have very... wait, I want to tell you everything. His father wants him to woo a very rich and aristocratic girl. You know how conniving the prince can be. Well, he insists on Alyosha marrying this girl and he'll do anything to make sure it happens because, well, he may not get another chance. Imagine, social position, a huge fortune, and I'm told that the girl is actually very pretty, well educated, with a good heart. Alyosha himself is quite taken with her. Well, his father wants to get Alyosha off his hands as quickly as possible so that he will be free to marry again himself. Well, naturally, the prince is determined to separate us in any way he can, because he is afraid that I have influence over his son."

"But is Valkovsky aware that you two are already in love with each other?" I asked, interrupting her.

"He knows everything."

"But who told him?"

"Why, Alyosha, of course. He told him everything."

"My God, what was he thinking? How could he tell his father, and at such a moment?"

"Now don't blame him, Vanya, don't laugh at him! You can't judge him the way you would anyone else. He's a child. A child who has been brought up quite differently from us. He's not aware of what he's doing. He's very impressionable, you see, and he tends to fall under the influence of the person nearest to him. The first bit of influence exerted over him is quite enough to cause him to renounce everything he believed just moments before. He has absolutely no strength of character. He is yours one day and later that evening he belongs to someone else. It's just the way he is, and he'd be the first one to admit it. Why, he might do something perfectly dreadful and you wouldn't know whether to blame him or feel just perfectly awful for him. He is capable of great self-sacrifice, but only until the next impression, and then he forgets all about it. And he will forget me too if I'm not always with him!"

"It's very possible, Natasha, that this proposed marriage is just a rumor. Do you really want to marry such a child?"

"His father is quite capable of such scheming."

"And how do you know this girl is so wonderful and that Alexey is taken by her?"

"He told me so himself."

"What? He told you that he might fall in love with another girl and demands that you sacrifice everything to stop him?"

"No, no, you don't know him! You haven't been with him enough to understand. You have to spend more time with Alyosha before you can make judgments about him. There is no one alive who is more honest or has a purer heart. It would be so much easier for me if he were a liar. I wouldn't be so drawn to him. It's not at all surprising that he should be attracted to her. If he were to spend a week without seeing me, he would probably go and fall completely in love with her... or someone else. But just as soon as he saw me, he would be all mine again. You see it's a very good thing that I know this about him because, if I didn't, I would simply die of suspicion. That's why I have decided, Vanya, that I must be by his side always, constantly, every moment, or he will forget about me and leave me! I understand him, Vanya, and without me every woman he sees might try to seduce him, and then what would happen? I would die! And, of course, I would be happy to die because what would life be without him? Worse than death, worse than torture. Oh, Vanya, you must see now how deeply I love him if I'm willing to leave my father and mother for his sake. You can't persuade me with your words because I am quite determined. I must have him by my side every hour, every minute! I can't go back now or I am lost! I know that!"

She stopped suddenly, then cried, "Oh, Vanya, what if he really has stopped loving me? If what you've just said is really true, that he is simply deceiving me..."

I had not said anything of the kind.

"If he was only pretending to be honest and sincere, but was really wicked and vain! And here I am defending him against your arguments when he may be with some other girl right now, laughing at me! While I, horrible, horrible creature that I am, have left everything behind and am searching about the streets looking for him. Oh, Vanya!"

Her agonizing moan was so painful that it saddened me to the depths of my soul. I could see now that Natasha was unable to control herself, that a blind, irrational jealousy had so taken hold of her that only the most insane, irrational solution was available to her. But another kind of jealousy, in my own heart, flared up and compelled me to say things that I knew would be hurtful. "I don't understand how you could continue to love him after what you've just told me. You have no respect for him, you don't believe he really loves you, and yet you are still willing to throw your family aside and run off with him. Your love has blinded you to reality; it has taken possession of you. I don't understand that kind of love."

"Yes, I love him insanely," she answered, as if in great pain. "You have never known such love, Vanya. I know that I'm crazy, that I've lost my mind, and that this may not be real love, but it doesn't matter, it's the only kind of love I have. I've known all along, even in my happiest moments with him, that this can't last, that it will only cause me pain, but what can I do if the pain caused by him is the only thing that gives me pleasure? I know what to expect and how much I will suffer. He's told me that he loves me, but I know I can't believe it, not after what he's put me through in the past. I have no faith in his promises; I don't trust his promises and never have, even though I know he has never lied to me and that he is incapable of telling a lie. I've even told him, Vanya, that I don't want to tie him down, that no one wants to be tied down, I'm the first to admit it, but I'd be happy to be his slave, a voluntary serf who'll do anything for him, if only I can have him with me, near me, and I can see him and look at him. It seems to me that even if he loved another, I could be happy knowing that he loves someone else, just as long as I could still be with him, by his side. How degrading is that, Vanya? How much further down can I go?" she cried, her eyes flaming with insane passion. "I know how demeaning this is and yet I know that if he abandoned me, I would run after him to the farthest reaches of the Earth, even if he hated me, and drove me away. You've tried to persuade me to change my mind and return, but I have no mind of my own. What if I did go back? I'd only run after him again tomorrow. He has only to snap his fingers, to whistle for me, and like his dog I would run after him at once. I'm not afraid of any torture, Vanya, as long as it comes from him. I just can't say it any other way!"

"And what about your father and mother, have you forgotten about them?" I thought to myself, but I only said, "Has he actually told you that he wants to marry you?"

"Yes, he promised, he has promised everything. He is coming to get me now and tomorrow we shall be married, quietly, somewhere outside the city, although he doesn't know where just yet. He doesn't understand these things, he's just as innocent as can be, but what an amazing husband he's going to be! It's funny, right? We'll be married tomorrow and, who knows, maybe the next day he will reproach me for it, but I don't want him to ever have anything to reproach me for. I don't ask anything from him. If his marrying me makes him unhappy afterwards, he is free to do what he wants."

"Natasha, you are delirious, you are so confused," I said. "Are you going to him right now?"

"No, he promised to meet me here and to take me away, we agreed." She looked eagerly along the street, but there was no one in sight.

"And yet he hasn't come. He's made you stand and wait for him," I cried with indignation. Natasha seemed shaken by the impact of my words and her face was painfully distorted.

"Maybe he's not coming at all," she said with a bitter smile. "He wrote to me three days ago and said that if I didn't promise to come tonight, he'd postpone our elopement to another day and that he would go with his father to visit his fiancée. Oh, Vanya, what if he really went to see her!"

I didn't answer. She held my hand firmly and her eyes sparkled.

"He is with her now," she said, so faintly that I could hardly hear her. "He hoped that I wouldn't come, so that he could go to her and say afterwards that it was my fault, since he had given me advance notice and I hadn't shown up. He's tired of me and is planning to leave me. Oh, God! I am so stupid! He told me the last time I saw him that I made him sick! Why am I waiting for him?"

"There he is!" I cried, suddenly jealous, as I saw him walking toward us along the embankment. Natasha trembled and cried out when she saw Alexey. Then she let go of my hand and ran to meet him. The street was nearly empty. They flew into each other's arms, and kissed and laughed. Natasha was laughing and crying at the same time, as if they hadn't seen each other for years. Her pale cheeks had turned crimson in her ecstasy. Alexey noticed me and immediately came over to me.

CHAPTER NINE

I looked at him closely. Although I had seen Alexey many times before, I now searched his face with a greater intensity, trying to understand what it was about him that puzzled me so, how a silly child like this could cast so powerful a spell over Natasha that it drove her nearly insane with love; a love so intense that she would recklessly sacrifice everything to worship at his shrine.

With both hands, Alexey clasped my hand warmly, and his clear, gentle expression immediately softened my heart. I knew that jealousy could cause a man to view his rival with unwarranted suspicion and I wanted to be as fair as possible. But I didn't like him and, knowing all that I did about him, I couldn't understand how anyone could fall in love with him, and yet it was clear that everyone else seemed to adore him. I didn't even like the way he looked, perhaps because he always dressed so elegantly, with a grace that seemed effortless to him. Later, I realized that my judgment was biased, but at the time I stubbornly refused to see beneath the surface. He was tall and slim, with a pale, oval face and blonde hair. His big blue eyes were kind and thoughtful, and sometimes, like gusts of wind, playful and childlike fancies would burst forth. His full red lips were perfectly formed and usually wore a serious expression, but when he laughed in that naïve, innocent way of his, it was impossible not to laugh along with him.

There were, of course, some minor flaws common to members of society: self-righteousness, frivolity, and a kind of polite insolence, but he was such a simple soul that he would be the first to acknowledge his faults and to laugh at them. His childlike honesty was so extreme that I don't think he could have told a lie, even in jest, unless he were entirely unconscious of it. Even when he behaved selfishly there was something so open and honest about his demeanor, so lacking in guile, that he never offended.

He was, however, weak and timid of heart, with absolutely no will or defenses of his own. To insult or lie to him would be as sinful as hurting a child, and his utter lack of knowledge of the world would probably not change in forty years. He seemed a perpetual child. Natasha instinctively felt that he could easily fall under the influence of another person but if he were persuaded to perform a bad deed, I think he would die of remorse upon learning of the consequences of his actions. But Natasha also understood that if she were to become his wife or mistress, she would start out as the queen of his heart and end as his victim. We often hurt the person we love most in the world, and Natasha knew that the rapturous joys of loving him would lead to madness and torment but she was, nevertheless, anxious to be the first to sacrifice herself.

Alexey's eyes sparkled with love for her and Natasha smiled at me in triumph. She had forgotten everything, parents, farewells, suspicions. She was happy.

"Vanya," she said, "I am guilty for doubting him. I thought you would not come, Alyosha, I doubted your love. Please forgive me for being suspicious and for being so unworthy," she implored, looking into his eyes with infinite love. He merely smiled, kissed her hand and then held it tightly in his.

Alexey turned to me. "Vanya," he said, "please don't blame me. I have been so anxious to greet you as a brother. I've heard such wonderful things about you from Natasha, and yet you and I have barely had a chance to speak to each other. Please, forgive me and be my friend," he said in a quiet, unassuming voice, and the blush on his cheek and the warmth of his smile immediately softened my heart to him.

"Yes, yes, Alyosha," Natasha cried. "Vanya is our dear friend and brother forever. He has already forgiven us and without that forgiveness we could never be happy. I have already told him that. Oh, you and I have been such wicked children, Alyosha, but the three of us shall be inseparable."

"Oh, Vanya," she continued, her lower lip trembling, "Go back home to them and let them know that you have forgiven me. It may not be so easy for them, but they love you, Vanya, and trust you, and when they see that you have forgiven me, maybe it will soften their hearts a little. Tell them everything, from the depths of your heart. You will find the words to make them understand. Be my defender and champion, protect me, save me! Why, do you know, Vanya, that I might never have had the courage to leave today if you had not stopped by? When I saw you, I felt in my heart that you would be able to soften the shock of my leaving them. You are my salvation. Go and tell them, Vanya, that I understand it won't be easy for them to forgive me, but at least convince them not to curse me, or God Himself will never forgive me. But if they do curse me, Vanya, let them know that I will continue to bless them and pray for them the rest of my life. They will have my love forever, even if I'm not with them. Oh God, why can't we all be happy?" she cried, suddenly, awakening to the truth of the situation. "After all, what have I done that is so terrible?" She buried her face in her hands.

Alexey quietly took her in his arms and held her tightly. There was silence for a few minutes.

I looked at Alexey reproachfully. "And you can allow yourself to make her your victim like this?"

"Don't blame me," he responded. "I can promise you that these troubles, as terrible as they may seem, will only last a minute, I'm sure of that. We just need to be strong for a little while to get through this ordeal. Natasha agrees with me. You know that it's just foolish pride, the family quarrel, the litigation, that are causing all the problems. But, I've thought about it, and I'm convinced that this will all end soon. Our parents will see how happy we are together and they will forgive us and each other. We will all be one big, happy family. Who knows? Maybe our marriage will be the start of their reconciliation. I don't see how it can be any other way. What do you think?"

"You talk about marriage, but when are the two of you planning to marry?" I asked, looking at Natasha.

"Tomorrow or the day after tomorrow. At least by the day after tomorrow. Maybe. You see, I haven't made any actual plans yet. I wasn't sure that Natasha would show up today and, besides, my father wants to take me to see my fiancée this evening. Natasha has told you, I hope, that he wants me to marry this girl, but that I don't want to. So I really couldn't be sure of anything happening today. In any case, it'll happen by the day after tomorrow, I'm sure of that, because things won't be the same otherwise. Tomorrow we'll head down the Pskov Road and stop in this village where a friend of mine from the University lives, a terrific fellow, you may know him. Well, at any rate, we'll find a priest in the village. I'm assuming there is a priest there, I probably should have checked on that first, but I didn't have the time. But this is all just detail. I'm sure we'll find a priest there, or in a village nearby. There's bound to be a priest around there somewhere, don't you think? I really should have taken the time to write my friend a letter and tell him that we're coming. He may not be home. Oh, but what does that matter? If we're determined to make this happen, it'll happen. In the meantime, Natasha will stay with me. I've rented a house for us to live in when we get back. I'm determined not to live with my father. You'll come and visit us, and our friends from the University will come, and it'll be like a reunion."

I think I must have looked a bit bewildered and sad, because Natasha gave me a glance that seemed to beg me to be tolerant. She had listened to his words with a sad smile, but with a look of proud admiration in her eyes, much as one might admire a little child's cheerful but nonsensical ramblings. I couldn't help but shake my head at him, though. It was very difficult to hold my temper.

"But are you really certain that your father will forgive you?" I asked.

"Of course, what else can he do? Except, maybe, curse me at first, he'll probably do that. He can be quite severe at times. He might even try to assert his legal power over me, as my father, but it won't be as bad as it sounds. He'll come around eventually, he loves me, and when he forgives me, Natasha's father will forgive her, and we'll all be happy again."

"But what if your father doesn't forgive you? Have you given any thought to that?"

"Oh, he'll forgive me. Maybe not right away, but I'll show him that I have character. He's often said that I have no character, that I'm too superficial, but I'll show him that I can take care of myself. And my wife, of course. Starting a family is no laughing matter, and I don't want to be thought of as a little boy anymore. He'll see that I have grown into a man and can support my family. Natasha tells me that that's much better than living at someone else's expense. She has a lot of practical ideas like that, things I've never thought of before. But I wasn't brought up to think... about things like that, I mean. But I did have an idea a few days ago, let me tell you about it, and Natasha should hear this too. I've decided to write stories and sell them to magazines the way you do. You can introduce me to publishers, can't you? And just last night I had an idea for a novel. I borrowed the idea from a comedy by Eugène Skrib. I think it could turn out splendidly. But I'll tell you about it later. The important thing is that my writing will bring in a lot of money. They do pay you, right?"

I couldn't help but laugh.

"You laugh," he said, and he laughed too, "but there is more to me than meets the eye. I have very astute powers of observation, you will see. You can test me yourself." He said this with the utmost sincerity. "Natasha is always telling me that I have so little understanding of the world, which is true, so I thought to myself, if I know nothing about real life, why not be a writer and just make things up."

Both Natasha and I were laughing now.

"Laugh," he said, "go ahead and laugh, but you'll see. And you'll help me, for her sake, because I know you love her too. I'll tell you the truth, Vanya, I know that I'm not worthy of her and I can't, for the life of me, understand what she sees in me, but I love her and would gladly give my life for her. Up till now, I haven't really thought about the consequences of her loving me, and I wasn't afraid of anything, but now I see that I am going to have to make some firm decisions and devote myself to taking care of her. But isn't it true, after all, that if a man is truly determined to do his duty, that he will find the strength and knowledge within himself to accomplish that task? And besides, I will have you to help me, as a loyal friend, and you know that I know nothing about anything, so there will be plenty for you to do. I hope you will forgive me for leaning on you in this way, but you are a much better man than I am, with a noble heart, and with your help I know that I can become worthy of both you and Natasha."

He clasped my hand again in both of his and the look in his eyes was brimming with such hope and assurance that I saw, clearly, that he believed me to be his friend.

"Natasha will help, too, and I know I will improve, so please don't think too harshly about me, and don't lose faith in us. I am confident that we'll have no money worries. If my being a writer doesn't work out—and to tell you the truth I think it's a silly idea and only suggested it to see what you thought of the idea—I can always give music lessons. You didn't know that I was musical, did you? And I'm not ashamed to work for a living, if necessary. I'm open to all possibilities. I also have a lot of trinkets, knick-knacks, that I can sell, and that will provide us with living expenses for a while. And if all else fails, I can go into government service. My father would like that, he's been encouraging me for years, but I've always said my health is too unreliable for that kind of work. But when he sees that my marriage has made me so much stronger and more dependable, and that I am working for the State, he will be so proud that he will forgive us immediately."

"But Alexey Petrovich, have you taken even a second to consider what happened this evening in her home and how her parents will react to this?" I asked. Natasha was overwhelmed with grief by my comment, but I continued. "Have you thought about what is going on between *her* father and *your* father?"

"Yes, you're right, it's terrible. I have been thinking about that and I am devastated, but what can I do about it? I love her parents very much; they took me into their home and loved me like a son, and look how I am repaying their kindness. I can only pray that they will forgive us. And this quarrel, this lawsuit, you cannot imagine how terribly we both feel. We love each other so much and yet our fathers fight. If only they would resolve their dispute and become friends again. They really should, you know, and then everything will be all right. But I must say that you're really making me think about this. Natasha, what we're doing really is a terrible thing. I tried to tell you that before, but you insisted on going through with it. But, tell me, Ivan Petrovich, there must be some way to resolve this conflict, isn't there? If we love each other, why shouldn't we be able to convince them to care about each other? How can they resist our love? You would be surprised to learn that my father is really a very kind-hearted man. He spoke so tenderly to me this morning about my future, and now here I am betraying him, all because of a little misunderstanding. It's all so stupid, really. If he took the time to get to know Natasha, within half an hour he would consent to anything she asked." He looked again at Natasha with a tender, compassionate gaze.

"I've told him a thousand times," he continued, rambling on incessantly, "that he would love Natasha if he really knew her — after all, no one has ever seen such a girl — but he is convinced that she is some sort of seductress, and my first obligation is to clear her name of such misconceptions, and I will, I promise you. Oh, my Natasha," he cried excitedly, "the whole world will soon know you and love you as I do, and what more do we need to find happiness?

Beginning today, with God's blessing, we will bring peace, happiness and reconciliation to everyone, right Natasha? But what's the matter with you, are you all right?"

Natasha was as pale as death. She had been following his words attentively, but had been growing paler and paler and her eyes had clouded over until she had drifted into a form of trance from which Alexey had suddenly awakened her with his question. She looked around and then, quite unexpectedly, rushed into my arms. She pulled from her pocket a letter which she was careful to conceal from Alexey. It was a note to her parents she had written the night before. She gave it to me with such a look of despair on her face that the image of it will haunt me forever. I was made terrifyingly aware that only now, at this precise moment, had she finally awakened to the inescapable horror of her decision. She tried to say something to me, but no words came, and she fainted. I only just managed to catch her. Alexey too had turned pale from fright. He took a flask of whiskey from his pocket and gave her a sip, then he kissed her lips and fingertips. Within two minutes she had regained consciousness. Alexey hailed a nearby cab and I lifted Natasha into the carriage. She grabbed frantically for my hand, her feverish tears burning my fingers. The carriage started off and I stood there for a long while, watching as my happiness vanished in the distance, severing my soul in two. Then, slowly, I retraced my steps along the road to her parents' house. I have no memory of what I said to them, it was all such a blur.

So ends the history of my happiness and my love. I will now return to my interrupted story.

Chapter Ten

Five days after Smith died, I moved into his apartment. All that day I was unbearably sad. The weather was miserably cold, alternating between rain and snow. Only briefly in the early evening did the sun show its face, and a stray beam of light found its way through my skylight windows, peaking in like a curious visitor.

I was beginning to regret my decision to move here. The room was wonderfully large, but the low-hanging ceiling, the sooty, musty odor, and the vast emptiness of the space (in spite of the woeful furniture supplied by the landlord) required some getting used to. I thought that surely this room had contributed to Smith's poor health and I feared for my own.

The next morning I set to work organizing my papers. Having no briefcase, I was forced to use a pillow case to transport them and as a result they were badly crumpled and out of order. I settled down to work on my novel, but my head was filled with so many other things that the pen soon fell from my hand.

I moved to the window. It was dark and dreary outside, which only served to depress me even more. My head was filled with sad, morbid thoughts, and it occurred to me that I would die here in St. Petersburg. Maybe in the spring, I thought, things would improve. When the sunlight returns, life will bloom again and a visit to the fresh fields and forests of my childhood will draw me out of my shell. If only there were some spell or magic potion that would enable me to erase the memory of the past few years from my mind, I might be able to start anew. Perhaps, I thought, I should take up residence in some lunatic asylum where my mind could be flushed clean of its debris and I would awaken with a whole new brain filled with life, confidence and hope for a brighter future. But then I laughed. What would I do when I left the asylum and returned home, write more novels?

I occupied myself for the rest of the day with similar bleak and dismal thoughts. Natasha had sent me a note the day before and I had promised to visit her late this evening. When the time arrived for the appointment, I quickly pulled myself out of my melancholy mood and gathered my things together. Even with the rain and slush, I thought, getting out of the apartment could only serve to brighten my spirits.

When darkness fell, my apartment seemed to expand and grow even more spacious. The previous night I had imagined that I could see Jeremiah Smith in a corner of the room, sitting and staring at me as he had so many times in Mueller's shop, and at his feet was Azorka. But something happened this evening that greatly surpassed that nightmare. I must preface this story by acknowledging that my senses had been greatly altered by the nervous strain of the past few days and, in my depressed state of mind, strange images and bizarre thoughts combined to create what I would call a mystic horror, a petrifying fear of some indefinable and nonexistent terror that made a mockery of all the sane and reasonable arguments against it. That fear was growing stronger and stronger, becoming an irresistible fact, dreadful, monstrous and inescapable, and any attempt to reason it away was useless. The mind, in such moments, acquires a greater clarity and sharpness and the fearful melancholy that takes possession of the senses resembles that terror experienced by people who fear the resurrection of corpses in graveyards. Such was the state of my mind when the event in question occurred.

I remember that I was standing at the table with my back to the door. I picked up my hat and suddenly felt a creeping sensation up my spine. I felt with certainty that if I turned I would see Smith standing in the darkness with his hollow eyes and that toothless grin, silently laughing at me, his long, skeletal frame quaking from that laughter. The image of this ghost was vividly and distinctly drawn in my imagination and I had the overpowering conviction that this inescapable experience was really happening. At this moment, I thought I heard the door creaking open. I turned quickly and stared into the darkness. Indeed the door was open, just as I had imagined it. I let out a cry. For a long moment the threshold was empty and silent. There was a slight movement and I was suddenly aware of a strange being whose eyes, gradually discernible in the darkness, were examining me closely and steadily. An icy chill ran through my body. The creature moved slowly in toward the light and I recognized the figure of a child, a young girl, and had the apparition been Smith himself it could not have been more frightening or strange than the appearance of this unexpected stranger at this late hour.

She had opened the door so slowly and quietly that it was clear she was afraid to enter. She took a few steps toward me without making a sound. I could see now that the girl was about twelve or thirteen, small, very thin, and so pale that she looked like she had only recently recovered from a serious illness. Her dark eyes flickered brightly in the candlelight. In her left hand she held a tattered shawl which she clutched tightly over her chest. Her dress was little more than rags and her thick black hair, soaked from the rain, clung to her face and shoulders. We both stood for several minutes examining each other.

"Where is Grandpa?" she asked finally, her voice hoarse and barely audible.

With this question, my terror instantly vanished. Upon closer examination I could see her resemblance to Smith. "Your grandpa?" I asked. "He's dead."

I instantly regretted the hastiness of my answer, but before I could say anything the girl began to tremble. Within seconds her shaking became so convulsive that I was afraid she would injure herself. I ran forward and grabbed her before she collapsed to the floor, holding her tightly for several minutes until her seizure had passed. As soon as she recovered, she made an unnatural effort to toss off the incident as a minor concern and pulled away from me.

"Forgive me, please, little girl, I'm so sorry. I didn't mean to... to announce it so abruptly, to shock you in that way. But maybe... maybe I'm wrong. Who are you looking for? The old man who lived here?"

"Y-y-yes," she whispered with considerable effort.

"Was his last name Smith?" I asked.

"Y-yes."

"Oh, well, then I'm afraid it's true," I said. "He died a few days ago. But please, don't be sad, don't cry. Why didn't you come sooner? Where have you come from? They buried him yesterday.

He died suddenly, quite unexpectedly. So, you're his granddaughter?"

The girl did not respond to my barrage of questions, but turned in silence and quickly moved toward the door. I was so surprised by this I didn't know what else to say.

She stopped in the doorway and without turning to me asked, "Azorka is dead too?"

"Yes, Azorka is also dead," I answered. It then occurred to me that this was a strange question, as if the girl were somehow confident that Azorka would just naturally die at the same time as the old man.

After hearing my answer, the girl quietly closed the door behind her and moved down the hallway to the staircase. After a moment I ran after her, upset with myself for letting her get away. I stopped at the top of the spiral staircase and listened for the sound of her footsteps, but hearing nothing I darted down after her. I had neglected to bring a candle with me and as the stairs were always dark and dirty, quite common in old buildings with small apartments, I had to grope my way carefully down the curving staircase to the fourth floor. From there the stairs descended to the ground floor in a straight line and I could see no one below me. I stopped to catch my breath and instinctively felt a presence behind me in the dark. I felt around in the blackness with my hands and came upon the girl, cowering against the wall in a corner of the stairwell. She turned her face to the wall and began to cry.

"Look, what are you afraid of?" I asked. "I didn't mean to scare you. It's all *my* fault. Your grandfather, when he was dying, mentioned you. They were his last words. I have a book he left behind, I think it's yours. What's your name? Where do you live? He mentioned the Sixth Line on..."

But I didn't get to finish my thought. She cried out in terror (perhaps because I knew where she lived) and pushed me aside with her tiny, bony hand, then rushed down the staircase. I hurried after her and heard the sound of her feet on the steps. Suddenly the sound stopped. When I reach the bottom of the stairs I rushed out into the street, but there was no sign of her. I ran up to Voznesensky Avenue where Mueller had his shop and searched both directions in vain. She had disappeared. She was probably hiding on the stairs when I ran past, I thought, and left the building after me.

CHAPTER ELEVEN

This was to be an evening of most unexpected encounters. The pavement on Voznesensky Avenue was wet with black slush and I had to dart quickly out of the way of a passer-by as he hurried down the street, his head bent down, apparently deep in thought and quite unaware of my presence. I caught a brief glimpse of his face as he passed and was astonished to recognize Nicolai Sergeich. The old man had taken to his bed three days earlier, seriously ill, so meeting him on the street in such damp, miserable weather was a great surprise, made even more so by that fact that he rarely left his home in the evening. Moreover, since Natasha had left home nearly six months earlier, he had become a virtual recluse.

When I called his name, he stopped and seemed delighted to see me, taking my hand in his strong grip. Without asking where I was headed, he steered me in the direction he was going and hurriedly pulled me along with him.

"Where is he off to?" I wondered to myself. Asking him, I knew, would be a wasted effort because he had grown so irritable in recent months that I was sure he would regard my innocent question as an insult or some shaded hint that he was doing something he shouldn't. As we hurried along the street I stole a glance at him. He had lost a great deal of weight and his beard was shaggy and untrimmed. The hair sticking out from under his crumpled hat and hanging down over the collar of his worn-out overcoat had turned surprisingly grey. I have noted before that the old man had grown absent-minded and forgetful and would sometimes sit alone in his room and talk out loud and gesticulate with his hands as if in conversation with another person. It was difficult for me to witness his declining mental health.

"Where were you off to, Vanya?" he asked. "I've been taking care of some business. How are you feeling?"

"I should be asking you that," I responded. "You were terribly sick just a few days ago and here you are up and about in this terrible weather."

As I expected, the old man did not answer me.

"How is Anna Andreyevna feeling?" I asked.

"Fine, fine," he responded, "although she's a little under the weather too. She's been feeling a bit low. She often speaks about you and wonders why you don't come to visit us anymore. Maybe you were on your way there right now, perhaps?" He looked at me suspiciously. "Or maybe I'm keeping you from something else, you have other plans?" He had suddenly grown irritable and distrustful and I attempted to avoid an argument by telling him that I was, indeed, on my way to visit Anna Andreyevna (although I knew this would make it too late for me to keep my appointment with Natasha).

"Well, that's good, very good, Vanya," he responded, evidently much relieved by my answer. He calmed down and continued our walk in silence.

A few minutes later he mechanically repeated, "Yes, that's very good," as though waking from a deep thought. "You see, Vanya, God did not bless us with a son and Anna Andreyevna and I have long felt that He sent you to us. I have always considered you my son and the old woman feels the same way. You have always been most respectful and tender towards us, never ungrateful, and we bless you for that, Vanya, and pray that God will bless you and love you as we do." His voice was shaky and he took a moment before continuing.

"Have you been sick, Vanya?" he continued. "Why haven't you been to see us for so long?"

I told him the story of my encounter with Jeremiah Smith and explained that his death and my subsequent illness had prevented me from paying them a visit. I almost mentioned that I had visited Natasha during that period but, fortunately, caught myself in time.

The old man was greatly impressed with my story about Smith and he listened with great interest. But when he learned that my new apartment was even damper than my previous one and that I was paying six rubles for it, he grew angry again. When he was in an irritable mood, his patience was extremely thin, and Anna

Andreyevna was usually the only person who could calm his temper (and even she was not always successful).

"It's that literature of yours," he said. "It's brought you to the garret and will eventually lead you to the cemetery. I told you it would, I predicted it. Is Belinsky still writing criticisms?"

"He died of tuberculosis. It seems to me that I mentioned that to you some time ago."

"Dead, is he? Dead! Well, that was bound to happen. Did he leave anything to his wife and children? I think you once said he was married. I don't understand why these people marry."

"No, he left her nothing." I said.

"Well, there you have it," he said dramatically, as if closing the subject. His concern for the deceased literary critic seemed as genuine as it would have been had he been discussing his own brother. "Nothing! How can there be nothing? But you know, Vanya, I predicted something like this would happen. He may have earned his place in history, perhaps even immortal fame, but such glory can't put food on the table. Like me, this man praised you and saw glowing things in your future, and then he died. But then, who doesn't have to die? And life is good and the world is a beautiful place and... Look there!"

With a suddenly unconscious gesture of his arm he pointed to a dim, fog-bound street illuminated by flickering gas-lamps, to the dirty houses, to the shining rain-soaked pavement, to the grim, angry and wet passers-by, all crowned by a solemn St. Petersburg sky, the totality of which created a vivid landscape as if drawn in India ink.

We walked on and soon arrived at St. Isaac's Square at the base of the recently completed cathedral, dark and ominous and barely discernible silhouetted against the somber sky. Towering above us was Montferrand's statue of Tsar Nicholas, rearing up on a magnificent steed.

"You have said to me, Vanya," the old man continued, "that this critic was a good man, magnanimous, personable, sympathetic, but let me tell you that there are many such men in the world and all they really know how to do is create more orphans. And yet I suppose that one should be content to die, anything to get out of this. Go anywhere, even to Siberia. It's bound to be an improvement. What is it you want, child?" he said abruptly, coming upon a little girl begging in the street.

She was tiny, perhaps seven or eight, dressed in tattered rags, with no stockings and battered old shoes on her dirty feet. Her dress, which she had clearly outgrown, was insufficient to protect her from the cold night air, but she did her best to hide the fact that she was shivering. Her pale, sick and emaciated face was turned up towards us and as she reached out her trembling hand her look was a timid, silent plea for kindness, mixed with an anticipation of rejection.

Ichmenyev immediately began to shake and he turned towards her with so sudden a movement that she stepped back in fear.

"What is it you want, little girl, don't be afraid. You want money?" he asked her. "Yes, well just a moment, this is for you, here, here, take it." He was quaking with emotion as he hurriedly explored his pockets in search of money. The few coins he drew forth were evidently insufficient to satisfy his generous spirit, for he then pulled open his purse and handed her a ruble note, which was all he had with him.

"May the good Lord Jesus watch over and bless you, my child, and may God's angels protect you!" He made the sign of the cross several times over the girl's head, but stopped suddenly when he realized that I was standing next to him. His mood changed abruptly and he frowned before quickly resuming his walk. I hurried after him.

"You see, Vanya," he said after a long, angry silence, "I cannot stand to see such tiny, innocent little children trembling from the cold in the street because of their cursed mothers and fathers. Could any mother send her child out to beg in the streets if she herself were not living in an equally wretched state? There may well be more future orphans huddled in a corner somewhere, with this one being the eldest, and the mother may be too sick to beg herself and..." He cut himself off abruptly. "Well, they are not princely children, Vanya, that is certain. There are many children in this world who are not the children of princes."

He was silent again and appeared reluctant to continue. When he spoke again he seemed embarrassed and a little confused.

"You see, Vanya, I have made a promise to Anna Andreyevna and we have both agreed that if the opportunity presents itself we will take an orphan, some small, helpless little girl, into our home and care for her. Life can get pretty boring for an old couple like us, living all alone, and lately Anna Andreyevna has grown restless and irritable. So I was hoping that you might have a little conversation with her. Don't say that I asked you to, of course, but make it sound like it's your own idea. Talk to her, feel her out on the subject. I've been meaning to bring this up for a while, but I haven't had an opportunity. It's just too painful for me to discuss it with her myself and, well, why should I? What's an orphan child to me, I don't need to deal with children at my age. It might be pleasant to have a child's voice in the house again, of course, but it's really to give Anna Andreyevna something to do, someone to take care of other than just me, and I think it would cheer her up a bit. Of course, it doesn't make a difference to me one way or the other, you understand, but, look, it's getting late, and the old woman is probably tired of waiting, so why don't we take a carriage?"

It was half past eight when we reached the Ichmenyev's home.

Chapter Twelve

The old husband and wife were very fond of each other. And love and long-term routine had created an inseparable link between them. But Nikolai Sergeich, not only now but in earlier, happier times, often found it difficult to express his feelings and would treat Anna Andreyevna in a manner that was, at least in the eyes of other people, downright unkind. In many respects he was tender and sensitive, but like others with similar temperaments, he found it difficult to express his gentler emotions and found it easier to mask these feelings behind an outwardly stern exterior, not only in public but in more private moments as well. Such was the case with Ichmenyev in his relations with his wife. He respected her and regarded her with the highest esteem (despite the fact that her only noticeable characteristic seemed to be that she was a good person and nothing more), and she in turn knew almost nothing about anything except how to love him, which she did simply and, perhaps, a bit too demonstrably.

If anything, their affection for each other had grown even stronger since Natasha had left home, and their awareness that they had no one in the world except each other for company made their bond even stronger. And while it is true that Nikolai Sergeich could become remarkably moody and irritable on occasion, the two were rarely ever apart and a separation for even as little as two hours could result in pain and depression for both of them.

There was an unspoken agreement between them not to speak about Natasha, and Anna Andreyevna was afraid to even hint at the existence of her daughter in front of her husband, although this was very difficult for her. She had forgiven Natasha in her heart long before and she and I would have private conversations about her lovely, unforgettable daughter whenever her husband was not in the room. She became positively ill if she didn't receive news from me and, when I did visit, her insatiable curiosity for every little detail was never satisfied. She became extremely agitated and fearful when I told her once that Natasha was sick (although not seriously) and very nearly rushed out to attend to her personally. But this was an extreme case. She wanted more than anything to go to her daughter, but feared her husband's angry reaction and suppressed these feelings when in his company. In private conversation with me, however, she spoke of Natasha in the warmest possible terms and always used affectionate pet names for her. She complained about her husband's bitter feelings toward his daughter and his stubborn unwillingness to forgive her. On occasion, when her grief became almost unbearable, she would find the courage to confront him directly and declare that God would never forgive his cruel and unconscionable lack of mercy, but that was as close as she ever came to dealing with the situation.

On such occasions, the old man became either sullen and quiet, retreating into himself, or aggressive and hostile, rising in anger and storming out of the room. Leaving the room I soon came to realize, was really his way of giving his wife an opportunity to vent her feelings to me, which she never failed to do, and for me to fill her in on the latest news about Natasha. Immediately after our arrival this particular night he declared, "I'm soaking wet! Why don't you sit down, Vanya, and tell Anna Andreyevna about your new apartment? I'm going to change my clothes," and without so much as a glance at either one of us, he hurried into the other room.

"There he goes again," his wife said. "He pretends that he has something to do, but he's really ashamed to express his feelings. He knows that you and I will talk about Natasha and he's purposely giving us the time to do that, but when he comes out again he'll pretend that nothing has been said. And it's so silly because he knows that I know what he's doing, so why does he pretend otherwise? There should be no secrets between us. He still loves Natasha and I know that he wants to forgive her, but he is too stubborn to admit it. I hear him crying at night, but the next morning his pride takes hold of him again and he hides his feelings. But tell me, Vanya, where did he walk to?"

"I was just going to ask you that," I responded. "I have no idea."

"I was so stunned when he left. On a cold, wet night like this, he never goes out unless it's for something very important, but what could be so important now? I'm afraid to ask. I keep hoping that he'll go to her, forgive her. He hears all the latest news about her and seems to know her every move, don't ask me how, but he never lets on, and he was very sad all day yesterday and this morning too. But Ivan Petrovich, have you nothing to say to me? I have been awaiting your return like the second coming and yet your eyes tell me nothing. What is that villainous man of mine planning? To disown Natasha?"

I immediately described to Anna Andreyevna everything I knew about the situation. As always, I was completely frank with her. There was something happening that might lead to a major rupture concerning Natasha's relationship with the young prince, Alexey Petrovich. Natasha had written begging me to come to her that very evening at nine o'clock, but I had been waylaid by Nicolai Sergeich just as I was leaving to visit her.

Prince Valkovsky, I explained, had returned two weeks earlier from a trip abroad and had immediately set to work solidifying his son's wedding plans. Alexey had been spending considerable time with his future bride and, from all reports, was beginning to fall in love with her. Natasha was extremely upset when she wrote the note and said that everything would be decided tonight, but failed to provide any further details. It was *imperative*, however, that she see me tonight.

"Go, Vanya, by all means, go. But first, have a cup of tea before he returns. Matreyna, where is the samovar? Matreyna! That girl is so slow. Yes, you'll have a cup of tea and then make some plausible excuse and go. And tomorrow, early, you'll come here and tell me everything. My lord, we don't have enough troubles already, what could be worse? He knows, I'm sure of it. Nikolai Sergeich knows everything that is going on. I think he gets the news from Matreyna. She has a god-daughter, Agasha, who works in the prince's house. You know how servants hear things. Well, Nikolai Sergeich was terribly angry this morning. He was screaming at Matreyna about money, and about this and about that, and you know when he is like that my feet go numb and my heart pounds. After lunch, he skipped tea and went in to take a nap, and I looked in on him—there is small crack in the door he doesn't know about—and saw him praying on his knees for a full hour. When he came out at five o'clock he grabbed his hat and coat and went for a walk. What does Natasha say in her note, may I read it?"

I showed her the note. For many years, Anna Andreyevna had held one cherished dream (which she confided only in me) that the young prince, whom she often referred to as a villainous, insensitive and foolish boy, would finally marry Natasha and that Prince Valkovsky would consent to the marriage and end the feud between the families. On no account would she dare to express such a thought openly while her husband was alive, although she knew that he suspected that she held such feelings and would reproach her in an indirect manner. Her greatest fear was that if he learned of the possibility of such a marriage, he would curse Natasha and cast her from his heart forever. We all held this belief and knew that if Nikolai Sergeich were ever to forgive Natasha it would be on the condition that she return home, repentant and having severed her relationship with Alexey completely.

"He's a cowardly, spineless boy," Anna Andreyevna said. "I have always thought so. He's like a weather vane that spins this way and that, depending on how the wind blows. I'm not surprised to hear that he is now enthralled by another woman."

"I have heard, Anna Andreyevna," I objected, "that his fiancée is a very charming girl. Yes, even Natasha has said very nice things about her."

"And you believe that?" she cried. "Charming? You writers think any pretty young girl who flips her skirt in your direction is 'charming.' And if Natasha says so, it's only because she is a sweet, noble soul who will readily forgive the sins of others while she herself suffers. Oh, these villains with their arrogant pride. Look how much Natasha has given up for him and he blithely moves on to the next girl. If only my husband would forgive her and bring her home. Has she lost weight?"

"Quite a bit, yes."

"My poor little girl. And we have such new troubles of our own, Vanya, I spent last night and all of today crying. I'll tell you about that some other time, but let me tell you how often I have been on the brink of begging Nikolai Sergeich to forgive our little girl, but I am so afraid he might curse her. Curse her! God himself is unforgiving to children whose parents curse them, so I live each day in terror of what he might do. And you, Vanya, who grew up in our home, you know that he was never unkind to you for a moment, and you come here and tell me that this other woman is 'charming?'

But Matreyna knows better. She knows the inside story. Prince Valkovsky, she says, is involved with a countess who for many years, even when her husband was still alive, behaved appallingly while living abroad. After she became a widow she scandalized Europe. The Italians and Frenchmen were practically fighting her off and there were several barons who were pursuing her, but she hooked onto the prince. Well, she went through her share of the family estate in no time, but the countess has a stepdaughter by her first husband who received two million rubles when her father died. Through proper investments, her fortune is said to be worth over three million now.

"The prince is no fool," she continued, "and he's not one to let such an opportunity pass him by, so he decides to marry this heiress off to his son Alyosha. Another of his relations, a count who helped educate the boy, agreed that three million rubles is no laughing matter and suggested that the prince go to the countess and make the proper arrangements. But the countess will have none of it and fights tooth and nail against such a proposal. 'You are free to marry me,' the countess said to the prince, 'but my stepdaughter will most definitely not marry your son.' The stepdaughter is said to be an angel, a devout and obedient child, and will not go against her stepmother's wishes. So the prince tells the countess, 'Do not worry. You have exhausted your own fortune and have many debts, but if you convince your innocent and wealthy stepdaughter to marry my foolish but obedient son, we will be their guardians and will have legal control of the money. What good does your marrying me do without a source of income?' The prince is a clever man, indeed, and he convinced the countess to consider his plan. For the past six months she has refused to change her mind, but she and the prince recently went to Warsaw together and came away with an agreement. That is what I was told by Matreyna, who received the information, in the strictest confidence, from her source in the prince's house. Three million rubles. Yes, charming, indeed."

I was amazed by Anna Andreyevna's story. It was in complete agreement with the version I had recently heard from Alexey himself, who claimed that he was not interested in Katerina Fedorovna's money. But the young heiress was attracted to Alexey and became enthusiastic about the idea of marrying him. Alexey also told me that his father was planning to marry the countess, although the prince denied this publicly in order to avoid provoking the countess. I have already written that Alexey was very fond of his father, whom he admired and praised and believed in like an oracle.

Anna Andreyevna had been extremely irritated by my praise of the young prince's future bride and said, pointedly, "This 'charming' girl is not a countess, you know. Natasha would be a much better match. She is from a long and noble family and this other girl is merely the daughter of a brandy dealer. I had forgotten to tell you that yesterday the old man was rummaging through some old papers in his desk. He was sitting there, very serious, and I thought it best to keep quiet. But then he got irritated with me for not saying anything and called me over to join him. He showed me some documents and explained to me about our family histories. The Ichmenyev family can boast noblemen dating back to the reign of Ivan the Terrible and the Shoumiloffs were around in the time of Alexei Mikhailovich Romanov and are even mentioned in Karamzin's *History of the Russian State*. So you see, Vanya, we are in no way inferior to others. I'm not sure why he chose to tell me all this now, but I think he was offended by the insulting comments made about Natasha. They have nothing over us except their money, and that greedy bastard of a prince runs after it like the thief he is. Everybody knows this. Is it true that he became a Jesuit while he was in Warsaw?"

"Foolish rumor," I answered, although I was struck by how pervasive this rumor had become. But hearing about Nikolai Sergeich exploring his family history interested me greatly. He had never before boasted about his pedigree.

"They are all villains and thieves," continued Anna Andreyevna. "But tell me about my Natasha, my dear friend, is she grieving, does she cry? Ah, but it's time for you to go to her! Matreyna! Matreyna! She's an unreliable girl. But say something, Vanya."

What was there for me to say? The old woman began to cry. "You mentioned some new troubles before. May I ask what they are?"

"Oh, Vanya, my cup of troubles is not yet empty," she cried. "I had a locket with a childhood portrait of Natasha in it. We had met an artist while traveling once, a very fine painter, and Nikolai

Sergeich paid him to create a portrait of our little girl, she was just eight years old at the time. The artist painted her as a little Cupid, with curly blonde hair, and a lovely little see-through muslin dress. She was so pretty, so very pretty, and I asked him to draw in little wings, but he refused to change it. Well, Vanya, after all these misfortunes began, I took the locket from its box and attached it to the same ribbon that holds my cross so I could wear it next to my heart. I was so afraid that Nikolai Sergeich would see it and throw it away or burn it like he has with so many of her other things. There is nothing left of Natasha in the house but this one little souvenir, and I used to take it out and look at it, yes, and even talk to it, when he wasn't around. I would bless it at night and when I spoke to it I seemed to hear Natasha speaking back to me. It's difficult for me to tell you this, but that locket was the one thing in my life that comforted me and I was so glad that my husband didn't know about it. And then, yesterday morning, it wasn't there! It had disappeared. I thought maybe I had dropped it and I searched and searched for it. I tore off the bedcovers, I looked everywhere, everywhere. And then I thought, maybe *he* found it! Or Matreyna. I knew it couldn't have been Matreyna because she would have returned it to me. She is devoted to me with her entire soul. Matreyna! When are you bringing in the tea? And then I worried, 'what will happen if *he* finds it?' I became very depressed and would sit by myself and cry and cry, the tears wouldn't stop. But then Nikolai Sergeich began acting so much more affectionate, yes more affectionate, with me. He would look at me, sadly, as if he knew very well what I was crying about, and he pitied me. And I started thinking, what does he know? Maybe he found the locket and threw it out and is feeling guilty about that. I had already searched outside the window and I had Matreyna search again but she found nothing. Maybe he threw it in the river, I thought, and cried all night long. It was the first night I was not able to bless it, and I feared that this was a sign of some great calamity, some great harm. It was clearly a bad omen and I have been crying ever since, crying and waiting for you, my angel of God, to come and comfort me and ease my heart."

The old woman continued to cry.

"Oh, yes, Vanya, I forgot to ask you. When you spoke to Nikolai Sergeich, did he say anything about an orphan?"

"Why, yes, Anna Andreyevna," I responded, "he mentioned it to me on our walk here. He said that you had both agreed to take in an orphan girl and educate her."

"I did not decide, Vanya, he decided. Nor did I agree. What do I want with an orphan? She will only remind me of my Natasha. I have a daughter already and she will remain my daughter forever. Where does he come up with such an idea? If he thinks it will comfort me, he is wrong, or perhaps he thinks it's a way to banish memories of Natasha from his mind, by attaching himself to some new child. What did he say to you earlier? What was his mood like, did he seem angry? Wait, I hear him coming, you can tell me some other time, but remember you must come back tomorrow!"

CHAPTER THIRTEEN

The old man came in and looked at us curiously as he sat at the table.

"Where is the samovar? Is the tea not ready yet?"

The moment Matreyna saw Nikolai Sergeich enter the room she hurried in with the tea, just as if she had been holding off until his return. She was an old, tested and loyal servant, but had an obstinate, stubborn personality, and was the most relentless complainer of any maid in the world. Although she was a little afraid of the old man and always spoke to him in the most respectful manner, Matreyna dearly loved the old woman but clearly held the dominant position in *that* relationship.

"Hmm, it's bad enough to come in soaking wet, but to have a servant who doesn't wish to serve the tea," he grumbled.

Anna Andreyevna immediately winked at me. Her husband could not tolerate these mysterious glances between us and pretended not to notice, but his eyes clearly acknowledged what had happened.

"The lawsuit is going very badly," he said suddenly. "I am going to lose the case. Because I don't have access to some very important papers I need and our inquiries haven't been properly filed. The charges against me are all lies but the prince knows how to manipulate the law to his advantage."

I didn't know how to respond to this statement, so I kept quiet. He looked at me suspiciously.

"Well, what's to be done about it?" he asked with a new surge of anger, irritated by our silence. "It's better it happens now than later. I'm not a thief, but if the court decides that I must pay, I will pay. My conscience is clear, so let it be on their heads. When I have lost everything I will sell what property we have remaining and move to Siberia."

"My God, why there?" his wife cried. "Why so far away?"

"What have we got closer that is better?" he responded rudely, welcoming the objection and, perhaps, hoping for an argument.

"Well, there are people," she began, looking at me for support.

"What people?" he shouted, his face turning red. "Thieves, liars, traitors? You'll find plenty of them in Siberia too, so you needn't worry there. But if you don't want to go with me, that's up to you, I'm not forcing you!"

"Nikolai Sergeich, how can you say such a thing?" she responded with great emotion. "I will go wherever you go. I have no one in the world but you except..." She broke off and looked at me again, imploring me to intercede, but I knew that when the old man was in this mood, anything I said to him would only anger him more.

Instead, I said to her, "Calm yourself, Anna Andreyevna, Siberia is not as bad as it may seem. If the worst happens and you need to sell Ichmenyevka, Nikolai Sergeich may be right about moving to Siberia. There you'll be able to find a good private home and..."

"Well, at least someone has something supportive to say," the old man roared. "We'll sell off everything and be on our way!"

"I never expected to hear such a thing from you!" she said to her husband, wringing her hands together. "And from you too, Vanya! You've had nothing but love and kindness from us, and now you..."

"Well, what else are we to do?" he interrupted. "When we have no money left, no home? Shall I go to Prince Peter and beg him to forgive me?"

When she heard the prince's name, the old woman began to tremble with fear. The teaspoon fell from her hand and landed on her saucer with a jangling sound.

"No, in fact that's an excellent idea!" he continued, taking a stubborn, malicious joy in taunting his wife. "Don't you agree, Vanya? Why should I pack up and move to Siberia? Tomorrow, I'll put on my best clothes with a nice clean shirt, trim my hair and beard, I must look my best for such an important man. I may even buy a new pair of gloves, very stylish ones, and pay court to his highness. 'My lord,' I'll say, 'father of us all, please have mercy on your humble servants and forgive us. Give me a piece of bread. I have a wife and small children!' Is that what you want, Anna Andreyevna? Do you want that?"

"No, my dear, I don't want that. Please forgive me for speaking so foolishly, for making a nuisance of myself, and please don't make me cry," she pleaded, trembling more and more with fear.

I am sure that at that moment the old man's soul was struck a near fatal blow as he witnessed his wife trembling with uncontrollable grief, and I believe that his pain may have been even greater than hers. But he had been unable to resist. So it is with some tender-hearted people when their own grief and anger become unbearable, they must lash out at someone, often the very person they would least want to hurt. They find a strange sort of solace in their own misery. Women, for example, sometimes feel misery and resentment even when there is no cause for resentment or unhappiness. There are also many men, as in the case of Ichmenyev, who occasionally display this characteristic even though they are in no way weak or feminine in their outward appearance. The old man felt the need to quarrel as a way to relieve his own suffering.

The idea occurred to me at that moment that Anna Andreyevna may have been right when she suggested that he had made an effort to reconcile with Natasha. Under the influence of some heavenly guidance, perhaps he had set out to visit his daughter but had been diverted by some event or circumstance. Thus thwarted, he had returned home angry and ashamed of his weakness, and vented his feelings by attacking the person whom he suspected of sharing his desires and of influencing his feelings. By failing to provide Anna Andreyevna with the delight and joy of his noble intentions, he made her the victim of his wrath instead.

Whatever his state of mind a moment before, the sight of his wife trembling before him instantly shamed the anger out of him. He stood silently for a good minute and I tried not to look at her. As the silence stretched on, I feared that the tension in him was building again and would eventually have to explode, perhaps even in a curse.

"You see, Vanya," he said suddenly, "I didn't mean to say that, but the time has come, I think, to speak frankly, you know what I mean? I'm glad you're here because I want to say out loud, so you both can hear, that I have had it with all of this nonsense, the tears, the sighing. The fact is that what I have torn out of my heart, with blood and pain, will never again find a home in my heart. It is over and done. That was six months ago, Vanya! I am saying this openly and precisely so that there can be no misunderstanding," he added, keeping his angry glance focused on me and avoiding his wife.

"I repeat," he continued, "I have had it, I am through with it. There are people who think I'm a fool, a coward. They say I'm weak and the lowest form of scoundrel, that I have gone insane with grief. That's all rubbish! I have taken all of my sentimental feelings and wiped them from my memory. Yes! Yes! Yes! I have no memories!"

He leaped from his chair and banged the table with his fist, rattling his teacup.

"Nicolai Sergeich! Have you no pity for Anna Andreyevna? Look at what you've done to her," I said indignantly, unable to resist. But I was only adding fuel to the fire.

"Pity?" he screamed. "I have no pity because she has no pity for me! Do you think I'm blind to the plotting that goes on behind my back, in my own home, in favor of some slut of a daughter who is deserving of all the punishment and curses that could be inflicted upon her?"

"No, Nikolai, no," Anna Andreyevna pleaded. "Say anything you want, but don't curse your only daughter!"

"Curse? Curse?" he repeated, his voice growing louder and louder. "Yes, I do curse her, because I am the one who has been abused her." He turned to me and pointed at his wife as he spoke. "Every day, day and night, I must endure her resentful scolding, her demands, her subtle hints that I should go and beg for forgiveness... yes, yes, that's what she expects of me. She tries to soften my heart so I'll show a little pity! Look here, Vanya! Here is what that sinful daughter of mine has done to me! I am called a thief, a swindler!" He pulled a bundle of papers from the side pocket of his coat and tore through them looking for one particular page. Not finding it, he grabbed more sheets of paper from his other pockets, tossing them on the table one after another. In his haste, another item was caught up in the papers and fell hard upon the table. Anna Andreyevna let out a cry. It was the lost locket!

I could hardly believe my eyes. The blood rushed to the old man's cheeks and he gasped audibly as he realized what he had done. Anna Andreyevna stood, hands clasped in front of her, and looked imploringly at her husband. There was a glow in her eyes that radiated hope and joy. The blush on the old man's face told her everything. She had not been mistaken; the mystery of the missing locket had been solved!

She realized that he had found it, was delighted by his discovery, and had jealously secreted it away so that he could look, with undying love, upon the face of his beloved daughter. Like her, he had hidden it away and taken it out only when alone to talk to, ask questions of, and even imagine responses from. And in moments of excruciating sadness, he had fondled it and kissed the angelic image of his darling child, she to whom he had publicly denied forgiveness but instead cursed in front of everyone.

"My darling Nikolai, you still love her," she cried, forgetting that he had cursed her just moments before.

But immediately upon hearing her words, he grabbed the locket and with a look of insane fury in his eyes threw it on the floor and stamped upon it with his boot.

"Forever! Forever I curse you!" he screamed hoarsely. "I curse you forever!"

"My Natasha!" the old woman cried. "My baby girl, he is crushing her, crushing her with his boot! You tyrant! You unfeeling bastard!"

But when he heard his wife scream, the insane old man stopped, horrified by what he had done. He quickly reached down, retrieved the locket from the floor, and rushed toward the door, but before he had taken two steps, he fell to his knees and grabbed hold of the arm of the sofa for support. He wept like a child, like a woman, relentless sobs that nearly suffocated him as he gasped for air, inexorable tears that vibrated in his chest. This seemingly cruel old man had become a child in the blink of an eye.

No longer a man capable of curses, Ichmenyev was unashamed to reveal his feelings as his imprisoned emotions broke free. His rapturous love for his daughter became evident as he kissed her portrait over and over again, clutching to his lips the locket that only seconds before he had nearly crushed under his foot.

"Forgive her! Forgive her!" his wife cried as she bent over and embraced him. "Forgive her and bring her home! God will rejoice in your humility and mercy and welcome you on the Day of Judgment."

"No! No! Never!" he rasped. "Never, never!"

CHAPTER FOURTEEN

I was an hour late for my nine o'clock appointment with Natasha. She was living then on the fourth floor of a dirty merchant house near the Semenovskaya Bridge over the Fontanka River. Originally, after leaving her parent's house, she had lived with Alexey in a small, but beautiful and comfortable third floor apartment near the Foundry, but the young prince had quickly depleted his capital. As a music teacher he was a dismal failure and he soon began to build up large debts. His initial funds went to furnish the apartment and to buy presents for Natasha, although she implored him, often with tears, to be more prudent with his money. But Alexey had a simple and sensitive heart that delighted in giving Natasha pleasure, in making each day with her a holiday. Sometimes he would spend an entire week planning and building up to some new surprise, teasing her and providing hints that would increase her anticipation. But such efforts were usually met by bitter recriminations from the object of his generosity and the result would be arguments and fighting.

Alexey was also spending money in ways that Natasha did not know about at the time. His school chums proved a bad influence on him and he would join them on excursions with a Minna or Josephine and he would fall in love for a night and then return to Natasha with the dawn, as much in love with her as ever. But such love carried an element of self-loathing as well. He would often come to me, depressed and tortured, and protest that he was unworthy of Natasha's love, that he was useless and evil. He couldn't understand why she loved him when he was such a child. He was partially right, of course. They were a badly matched couple. He behaved like a child and she treated him like one.

With tears in his eyes, Alexey would tell me about his various sexual escapades and beg me not to tell Natasha. On such occasions, Alexey would go to Natasha (dragging me along with the hope that my presence would soften her heart) and make some timid effort to confess, but she would immediately see through him. Although clearly jealous, Natasha would immediately forgive what she called "his little eccentricities." This was not any kind of pretense on her part, for this exquisite creature truly delighted in forgiving and pardoning her Alyosha and she felt there was something subtly charming about her act of forgiveness.

There was one instance when Alexey, upon receiving Natasha's unqualified forgiveness, burst forth like a fountain with joy and rapture, and with tears of happiness, hugged and kissed her, and then proceeded to narrate his recent adventures in the arms of Josephine in the minutest detail and with such childish frankness, that Natasha ended up laughing along with him. The evening ended quite happily with the two entwined in each other's arms.

When Alexey ran out of money, he began to sell things. Natasha insisted that they move to a smaller, less expensive, apartment on the Fontanka and once there they continued to sell off their possessions. Natasha even sold some of her dresses and began to look for work. When Alexey found out, his despair knew no limits. He cursed himself, swore that he hated himself, and then proceeded to do nothing whatever to improve the situation. Soon it became clear that Natasha's meager earnings would prove their only reliable financial resource.

When they first began living together, Alexey had a major fight with his father. The prince's plan to marry his son to Katerina Fedorovna Filimonova, the stepdaughter of the countess, was still in its infancy, but he was determined to carry through with it. He had taken Alexey to visit his proposed bride and encouraged the boy, with considerable cunning and not a little bullying, to woo Katya and win her heart. When this effort was thwarted by the countess, Valkovsky decided to ignore his son's relationship with Natasha for the time being, and direct his efforts to charming and pleasing the boy in order to maintain his love and loyalty. Alexey's infatuation for Natasha, he decided, would soon dissipate on its own, long before any marriage could take place. The young couple would not leap into marriage without first securing his own consent and their own financial solvency. And Natasha showed no inclination toward even discussing the subject.

Alexey, in private conversation with me, assured me that his father was quite happy with the situation and, in fact, enjoyed the fact that it upset Natasha's father. But in reality, the prince continued to show his dissatisfaction with Alexey and proceeded to reduce his son's already scant allowance even more (he had never been particularly generous to begin with), and threatened to cut the boy off entirely. However, about this time, the prince traveled to Poland with the countess, determined in his own sly way to pursue his pet project. Alexey was too young for marriage, perhaps, but his future bride was very wealthy, and to overlook such an enviable virtue was unthinkable. Valkovsky soon decided to speed things along. Rumors began to spread that Alexey was engaged to marry the young heiress and when the prince returned to St. Petersburg he greeted his son most warmly. But when he discovered that Alexey was still intent on marrying Natasha, he was shocked and soon ordered his son to break off the relationship.

Valkovsky quickly came up with an even better plan, however, and took Alexey with him to visit the countess. Her stepdaughter was almost beautiful and almost still a child, but she had a warm, generous heart, a pure, unblemished soul, and a cheery, witty and tender disposition. After six months with Natasha, Alexey's passion for her will have surely lost its novelty, the prince decided, and Katya, seen through fresh eyes, will most certainly seem all the more attractive.

The prince was only partially correct. Alexey was attracted to the girl, but he saw that his father's unusually engaging personality was feigned and only served to camouflage his cold and calculating manipulations. But the value of this information was offset by the charms of Katya, whom he was now seeing every day.

When I headed for Natasha's apartment, I knew that she had not seen Alexey for five days. I was very concerned about what she would have to say to me. Even from afar, I was able to distinguish the candle burning in her window. Some months before we had agreed that if there was a candle in her window, it meant she wanted to see me. That way, if I was walking by (which I did nearly every night) and saw the signal in the window, I would know that she was waiting for me and that I was needed. Recently, the candle had been on display quite often.

CHAPTER FIFTEEN

I found Natasha alone. She was quietly pacing back and forth across the room, deep in thought, with one hand on her chest. The samovar was boiling on the table; she had prepared the tea for me much earlier. When she saw me she smiled silently and held out her hand. Her face was pale and in her expression I saw a tender, patient kind of anguish. Her clear blue eyes seemed even larger than usual and her hair appeared thicker, perhaps because she had lost so much weight.

"I was beginning to think you weren't coming," she said, taking my hand in hers. "I was about to have Mavra go and look for you. I was afraid you were sick again."

"No, I'm not sick. I was delayed. I'll tell you about it later. But what's happened with you, what is it?"

"Nothing," she answered calmly, as if surprised by my question. "What do you mean?"

"You wrote to me yesterday and asked me to come see you. You begged me to arrive precisely at nine o'clock, not one minute earlier, not one minute later. That's not your typical invitation to tea."

"Oh, yes. I was expecting him yesterday."

"And did he show up?" I asked.

"No," she said. She took a moment before continuing. "And I thought, if he doesn't show up, I'll have something to discuss with you."

"Are you expecting him tonight?" I asked.

"No, he spends his evenings there."

"What are you saying, Natasha? Do you think he may never return?"

"Of course he will," she said, with a very serious expression. The speed with which my questions were assaulting her made her uncomfortable.

She was quiet again and we walked about the room in silence. After a few minutes, she stopped and smiled. "I've been waiting for you a long time. Do you know what I've been doing to pass the time? I've been pacing about the room reading poetry. Do you remember the poem 'Sleigh Bells?' We used to read it together, remember?

"The storm has passed, the sky is clear,
I await the sound of his sleigh.
When the sleigh bells ring, my love will appear
And I'll welcome the light of the day.
The frosted glass on the window pane
Is aglow like a twinkling star.
The room is warmed by the morning sun
And the steam of the samovar.

"Such lovely verses, Vanya. What a pretty picture they paint, like an embroidered tapestry. I can picture the house in my head, very much like the one we grew up in, with the cotton curtains and the roughhewn log beams. The woman waits with such patience and tenderness for her lover. It all seems so comforting, and yet, so sad at the same time."

She became silent for a moment. Her hand went to her throat, as if suppressing a sigh.

"You are such a good friend, Vanya," she said after a moment and then became quiet again. Clearly, she had something to say, but had either lost her train of thought or couldn't find the right words. Meanwhile, we continued to pace about the room. In one corner there was a lamp illuminating a portrait of Jesus, which struck me as odd since Natasha had not been particularly devout lately.

"Is tomorrow a holiday?" I asked.

"No," she answered sharply. Then, more calmly, she continued, "No, it's not a holiday. You must be tired, Vanya. Sit down. You haven't had your tea, have you?"

"Yes, I've had tea," I said. "But let's both sit down."

"You had tea before? Where have you just come from?"

"From them," I said. We always referred to her parents as "them" and to their house as "there."

"From them? What time did you go there? Did you just happen to stop by or did they ask you to come?" She bombarded me with more questions and her face grew paler the more agitated she became.

I described every detail of my encounter with her father, my conversation with her mother, the scene with the locket, everything in the greatest of detail. I kept nothing from her. She listened intently, devouring my every word, and tears sparkled in her eyes. She was particularly agitated when I told her about the incident with the locket.

"Wait, wait," she cried frequently, interrupting my story and imploring me to recall even greater details about what had happened and what was said. I went over many of the details a second and third time until she was finally satisfied that there was nothing more to learn. "And do you really think he was coming to visit me?" she asked when I had finished.

"I don't know, Natasha, I can't even begin to guess. What's clear is that he misses you very much and is miserable without you. But whether or not he was on his way here is..."

"And did he really kiss my portrait in the locket?" she interrupted. "Did he say anything when he kissed it?"

"I don't know, Natasha, most of it was just incoherent mumbling, but he did use many affectionate pet names for you."

"Pet names? Affectionate?"

"Yes." I said, and she began to cry softly.

"My dear papa," she said, and after a few seconds added, "He knows about everything, you know, so I'm not all that surprised. He knows all about Alyosha, where he goes and whom he sees."

"Natasha," I said timidly, "Let's go to him..."

She instantly started to rise from her chair but stopped herself. "When?" she asked. She must have thought I meant immediately.

"No, Vanya," she added, clasping me by the shoulders with both hands. "We've talked about this many times. Let's have no more of it."

"But do you really mean to say that you won't make any attempt to end this silly feud?" I asked, feeling very discouraged. "You can't be so pig-headed that you won't even consider making the first move! That's probably all the excuse your father needs to give in and forgive you. He's your father, Natasha, he loves you. But he was very hurt and you have to pamper his pride a little. It's your duty as his daughter, and it's the right thing to do. Just make an effort and he'll forgive you unconditionally."

"Unconditionally, that's not possible! And don't reproach me, Vanya, it's not necessary. I have thought about it, day and night. In fact, there hasn't been a day since I left home that I haven't thought about it. You know very well that we've talked about this many times, but you also know, as well as I do, that it's just impossible."

"At least try."

"No, my friend, I can't. Even if I did try it would only anger him more. We can't turn back the clock, Vanya. We'll never be able to relive those blissful days when we were children together. Even if he were able to forgive me and allow me to come home, he wouldn't know me anymore. He loved another girl, a large child. He delighted in my childlike innocence, and when he hugged me and patted me on my head it was like I was still a seven-year-old sitting on his knee and reciting nursery rhymes. From my earliest childhood to the day before I left home he would come into my room at night and bless me. A month before I left, he bought me a pair of earrings and made a big show about keeping them a secret from me, but I found out about them anyway. He was like a little boy imagining how delighted I would be when he gave me the earrings, and then, when he found out that I already knew about them, he became so outrageously angry. And just three days before I left, he saw how depressed I was. What do you think his solution was? He bought tickets to the theater! My God, he thought that theater tickets would instantly cure me! I say it to you again, Vanya, he knew and loved a little girl, and never thought for a moment that I might actually grow up to be a woman. It never even occurred to him. So what good would it do for me to go home? He wouldn't know me.

"And if he *did* forgive," she continued, "who would he be forgiving? Not the person he would greet when I returned. I'm not a child; I have lived through too much to be called a child. Even if he liked the person he met, he would forever be lamenting the loss of the happy child he had known. The past always seems so much rosier until you really think about it, then it becomes torturous." She caught herself and added, "Oh, but I didn't mean our past, Vanya," but she left a pain in my heart nonetheless.

"Everything you say is true, Natasha," I said. "But it just means he'll have to get to know the *new* you, and he'll fall in love with you all over again. You really can't believe that a good man like your father wouldn't be able to observe and understand you, in his heart."

"Oh, Vanya, you're being difficult. There's nothing special about me to understand, that's not what I'm saying. My father is a jealous man. He is offended that my affair began and, perhaps, ended without his knowledge. Alyosha was there every day and he never saw our love grow. He didn't see it coming. I never went to him and told him how I felt, but kept everything from him. So when I ran away, he blamed it on my secrecy and saw it as a betrayal of his trust. I assure you, Vanya, it was the secrecy that offended him, not my love for Alyosha. When I ran off with my lover, he saw it as my deserting *him*! Even if he could take me back, that seed of resentment would remain in his heart and by the second day, by the third day, his dissatisfaction would grow into hostility and the quarreling would begin again.

"Let us assume, Vanya, that I do go to him and beg his forgiveness. I tell him, from the bottom of my heart, that I was wrong, that I understand exactly how much I have offended him and that I truly regret it. What if I tell him how much genuine suffering my 'happiness' with Alyosha has caused me, how miserably unhappy I have been, that I am almost choking on my pain. Even that would not be enough for him. He would demand more. He would require me to curse my past, curse Alyosha, and repent for the sin of falling in love. He would demand the impossible, that I wipe away the past six months and erase all memories from our minds. But I can't do that, Vanya. I will not curse anyone and I cannot repent. What happened is what happened and nothing can change that. No, Vanya, the time is not yet right."

"But will it ever be right?"

"I don't know. Maybe it'll be necessary to suffer even more before we can realize our future happiness. Suffering cures all. Oh, Vanya, there is so much pain in the world!"

I was silent and looked at her thoughtfully.

"Why are you looking at me like that, Alyosha?" she asked and then corrected herself with a laugh. "I mean, Vanya!"

"I'm looking at your smile, Natasha. Where did it come from? You've never smiled like that before."

"Why, what's different about my smile?" she asked.

"There is still a trace of your old innocence, but when you smile I seem to see something pulling at your heart. You've lost so much weight and your hair seems so much thicker, is that possible? And that dress you're wearing, it must have been made for you when you were living with them."

"Ah, you still love me, don't you?" she answered. There was a tender, affectionate look in her eyes. "Tell me how you are, Vanya. What have you been doing?"

"Nothing's changed," I said. "I'm still working on my novel, but it's not easy. Inspiration is elusive and ideas are difficult to pin down. But I'm still writing for a magazine, and I have to submit a specific number of pages every week without fail, so that keeps me busy. I'm considering giving up writing novels and dedicating myself to lighter material, something without a trace of gloom, no tears. Everyone seems to want to laugh and be cheerful!"

"Poor, Vanya, forever with your nose to the grindstone. But what about Smith?"

"Smith? He died a week ago."

"Yes, but hasn't he appeared to you in nightmares? I'm serious, Vanya. When you were sick, your nerves were frayed and I thought you might be having strange visions. It occurred to me when you told me about the new apartment you were renting. Is it still damp? It sounds like a dreadful, dreadful room."

"Well, yes. Actually, something did happen there this evening. But I'll tell you about it later."

She wasn't listening anymore. She seemed preoccupied with other thoughts.

"I don't understand how I could have left them like that," she said finally. "I was in such a fever." Her expression told me that she wasn't expecting an answer and she probably wouldn't have heard me if I had given one.

"Vanya," she said, her voice barely audible. "I asked you here for a reason."

"Which was?" I asked.

"I'm leaving him."

"You *have* left him or you *intend* to leave him?"

"I can't live like this anymore. I asked you here to tell you that, and to tell you about everything that has happened, even what I've kept hidden from you until now."

She often started like that, intent on revealing secrets to me, only to discover that I already knew them.

"Ah, Natasha, you've said that a thousand times. Of course, you can't continue to live together. You have nothing in common. You're much too different. But do you have the strength to leave him?"

"Until now it was just a thought, but now I've definitely made up my mind. I love him beyond measure, but I'm his worst enemy. I stand in the way of his future and I must let him go. He can't marry me and go against his father's wishes. I don't want to tie him down. I'm glad that he's fallen in love with another woman. It'll be easier for him to let me go. I see this as my duty. If I truly love him, then I must prove it by freeing him. It's my duty. Isn't that true?"

"But you've never done anything to force him to stay."

"No and I never will, that's not going to change. If he walked into the room right now, I would act just the same as always. But I have to find a way to make it easier for him to leave me with a clear conscience. That's what tortures me. Help me, Vanya, please, what should I do?"

"The simplest way is for you to fall out of love with him and in love with someone else. But even then, you can't be sure it'll work. You know how he is. He left you five days ago and may well have deserted you, but if you were to write him a letter and tell him you wanted out, he'd come running back immediately."

"Why do you hate him so?"

"Me?"

"Yes, you! You! You're his enemy, both secretly and openly. You can't even mention his name without sounding vengeful. I've seen it a thousand times; you enjoy degrading and insulting him. It's true."

"Well, if, as you say, I've done that a thousand times, there's no need to mention his name ever again. Let's change the subject."

After a moment of silence, she said, "I'd like to move to another apartment. Now don't get angry, Vanya."

"He'll find you no matter where you move," I said. "And damn it, I'm not angry!"

"Love is strong. Maybe his new love can hold him. Even if he did come back to me, it would only be for a minute, don't you think?"

"I don't know, Natasha, he doesn't seem capable of doing anything in a normal way. I think he wants to marry *her* and continue to love *you*, and in his mind, that's quite reasonable."

"If I could only know for sure that he really loves her, it would be so easy to make up my mind. Vanya, don't lie to me. Are you hiding anything from me that I should know about?" She looked at me imploringly.

"There's nothing, my friend, really. I give you my word. I'm always honest with you. But what I think is that he may not have fallen in love with the stepdaughter of the countess as strongly as it appears. So keep your spirits up."

"Oh my God, Vanya, do you really believe that? If I could only know for sure. I just wish he were here this minute so I could look in his eyes, then I'd know. He can't hide anything from me. But he's not here, he may never be here!"

"And yet you're here waiting for him, aren't you?"

"No, he's with her. I know because I sent someone to check on him. And, you know, Vanya, it may be foolish, but I'd really like to see her too. Is that possible, do you think? That we could meet somewhere?"

I had an uneasy feeling as I said, "Of course, you could see her. But just getting a look at her isn't going to do you much good."

"It would be enough for now. I could guess the rest. Listen, Vanya, I've been acting like an idiot, pacing up and down, up and down, just thinking about them, my brain is ready to explode. But here's a thought. You could meet her, couldn't you? The countess praised your novel, you told me so yourself, and you've been to a few of Prince Rudolph's society parties. You're sure to run into the countess there one night and she could introduce you to her stepdaughter. Then you could come back here and tell me all about her."

"Natasha, my dear, can we please talk about this later? Right now I want to ask you, do you really think you're strong enough to break up with Alyosha? Look at yourself, you look like death itself."

"I can take it," she said, barely audible. "It's for him. Everything I do is for him! But you know, Vanya, the one thing I can't stand is the thought of him sitting there with her right now, laughing and telling stories the way he used to here, and completely forgetting about me. He's staring into her eyes, the way he did with me, and not a single thought of me enters his head. He's not even thinking about me sitting here with you," she cried in despair.

"But, Natasha, only a minute ago you said..."

"We need to do it together," she announced, with a sudden burst of inspiration. "We have to break up at the same time! He'll have my complete blessing, of course, but it's just too difficult, Vanya, to imagine him just forgetting about me! Oh, I'm such a mess, I don't know what I'm saying. I *think* I'm being so calm and rational, but it's really not true. What's going to happen with me?"

"You'll be fine, fine, Natasha, calm yourself!"

"It's been five days, five days!" she continued. "Asleep or awake, all I do is think about him. It's always about him, about him. Oh, Vanya, let's go there now, take me there!"

"Calm down, Natasha," I begged her.

"No, let's go now!" she insisted. "I've been waiting for you for three days, so I've had plenty of time to think about this. That's what I was writing to you about. You must take me to him and you cannot refuse me. I've been waiting for you! Three days! There's a party at Prince Rudolph's tonight. He'll be there!"

She was delirious. At that moment, I heard a commotion in the hallway. Mavra was arguing with someone.

"Wait a second, Natasha, who's that? Listen!" She stopped to listen but there was a smirk on her face as if she doubted I was telling the truth. Then, suddenly, she turned pale.

"Oh, my God! Who's there?" she whispered.

She tried to hold on to me, but I hurried into the hall to see what was happening. As I feared, it was Alyosha, and Mavra was doing her best to prevent him from coming in.

"Oh, so now you show up," Mavra was saying. "Where have you been off to? If you want to wander, go wander, go! What have you got to say for yourself?"

"I'm not afraid of you or anyone! I'm going in there!" Alyosha sounded considerably more confident than he looked.

"I'm going to hurt you if you don't stop!" Mavra announced.

"Ah, there you are," he said as I came through the door. "I'm so glad you're here! Well, I'm here too, now. But how am I going to..."

"Well, come in," I said. "What are you afraid of?"

"I'm not afraid of anything, I can assure you. By God, I have nothing to feel guilty for," he declared, then added, "Do you think I should feel guilty? Well, you'll see how I explain myself to Natasha!"

He stood his ground and called out, "May I come in?" But there was no answer.

"What's the matter?" he asked me, his confidence quickly fading.

"Nothing," I said, and moved aside to let him enter.

Alyosha carefully stepped into the room and looked about timidly. There was no one there. Suddenly I spotted Natasha hiding between the cabinet and the window. She seemed neither living nor dead. When I think back on this scene, even now, I can't help laughing. Alyosha quietly slithered past me and toward her.

"Natasha! What's the matter? How are you? What's new?"

"Well," she answered, "nothing much." She seemed quite embarrassed and a bit guilty when she realized she was hiding in the corner. "Have some tea?"

Alyosha was confused and frightened. "Oh, Natasha! Maybe you're thinking that I'm to blame for something? Well, I am blameless, I am innocent! You'll agree when you hear what I have to say."

"But... Oh, what's the use?" Natasha whispered. She held out her hand to Alyosha, who took it. "Whatever you have to say, I'm going to forgive you, and things will end up pretty much the way they always do." The blush was beginning to return to her cheeks as she moved back into the center of the room. She kept her eyes on the floor, rather than looking at Alyosha.

"Oh, my God!" he yelled with enthusiasm. "If only I had been guilty of something, I wouldn't have the nerve to look you in the face again!" He turned to me. "But look here, she won't look at me. She thinks I did something wrong, just because of the visible evidence against me. Five days I was gone! She hears rumors that I am engaged to another woman, and yet she reaches out her hand to me and tells me that all is forgiven. Oh, Natasha, my dear, sweet angel, I am not guilty, and you know it! Quite the contrary. I am innocent. But you should be there! Right now. They have invited you to the party. What time is it?" He retrieved the gold pocket watch from his vest pocket. "It's half past ten. I've been there all evening," he continued, returning the watch to his pocket, "but I told them I wasn't feeling well and needed some fresh air. It's the very first moment I've had in five days to get away from them, and here I am running to you! I could have gotten here sooner, Natasha, but I purposely didn't come. I'll tell you why later, but you need to know that I am blameless. Completely!"

Natasha raised her head and looked at him. The expression on his face was so open and honest, so enthusiastic and caring, that it was impossible for her not to believe him. I half expected them to fly into each other's arms as usual, but Natasha seemed so emotionally overcome by her joy that she lowered her head again and began to sob quietly.

Alyosha would have none of it. He quickly kneeled before her and in a frenzy of passion kissed her hands and feet. Natasha's legs began to tremble visibly. I pushed a chair towards her and she fell back into it.

CHAPTER SIXTEEN

Within a minute or two the three of us were laughing like lunatics.

Alexey's voice rang out, "Please let me tell you my story! It's not at all like my other tales; this one is really interesting!" His words only prompted greater laughter from Natasha and me. "Aren't you ever going to stop laughing?" he cried. Clearly, he was determined to tell his story, but his comic indignation only added to our amusement. Natasha made an attempt to suppress her glee, but one look at Alyosha's childish pout set her off again. Like Gogol's Nozdrev, we had reached the point where Alyosha only needed to raise a finger to stretch our cheeks to their limits and set our stomachs to quaking.

Mavra, who had been working in the kitchen, came to the doorway and stood there with a sour expression. She had been expecting Natasha to give the young prince a severe scolding and was dismayed to discover that five days of separation had resulted in little more than unrestrained merriment.

Natasha at last realized that her high spirits were making Alyosha unhappy and she stopped laughing. "What is it you want to tell us?" she asked.

"Do you want me to bring out the tea?" interrupted Mavra, who had no respect whatsoever for the sullen young man.

Alyosha waved his arms and shouted, "Go away, Mavra! Get out!"

Mavra shook her head and retreated to her kitchen.

"I will tell you everything that has happened, and everything that is going to happen, because I know all about it. I imagine that you both want to know where I've been for the last five days. I will tell you, if you let me. Well, first of all, Natasha, I want you to know that I have been deceiving you. Not just this week, but before that."

"Deceiving me?"

"Yes, deceiving you, for an entire month, even before my father came home. The time has come for me to be completely honest. About a month ago, I received a long letter from my father that I kept a secret from both of you. In the letter he told me straight out, and in such a serious tone that it frightened me, that his matchmaking campaign for me had been successful and that he had found me a perfect bride. I was unworthy of her, he pointed out, but we were to be married anyway, so I had better accept that fact and clear my head of all the nonsense, and so forth and so on. Well, of course, we all know what 'nonsense' he's referring to, right? So, that's the letter I hid from you."

"Hid from me?" Natasha said. "That's ridiculous. The moment you received it you came here and told me everything. I still remember how you became such a sweet little boy, tender and obedient, like a puppy who had misbehaved. You wouldn't leave my side until you had revealed every fragment of the letter."

"That can't be!" Alyosha looked genuinely surprised. "Well, I probably didn't tell you the most important thing. You may have both guessed it, that's not my concern, but I know I didn't tell you. And I've been feeling terribly guilty about keeping it from you."

"I remember too, Alyosha," I said. "You came to us and described the whole letter in detail. I certainly didn't have to guess at anything." I looked at Natasha.

"You told us everything," Natasha added. "So stop bragging about your great skill at keeping secrets. Even Mavra knows all about the letter, don't you, Mavra."

"What's not to know?" Mavra replied, sticking her head back through the door where she had apparently been standing the whole time. "You told all three of us. Sly as a fox you're not."

"Oh, you're so aggravating! She's just trying to annoy me, Natasha. She wasn't even here when I told you. Don't you remember, Mavra, we didn't have any money then and I sent you to pawn my silver cigarette case? So you couldn't possibly have heard me. And even if you were here, you usually fall asleep when I'm speaking anyway! Natasha, you've done a fine job of training her, I must say. But let us all assume, just for the sake of argument, that I actually did describe my father's letter. What I didn't convey to you was the tone of the letter."

"Well, what about the tone?" Natasha asked, barely able to suppress a smile.

"Now look, Natasha, you may think this is all a joke, but it's no joke I can assure you! This is very important. My father had never before spoken to me in such a tone, a tone that stunned me, as if the whole city were collapsing around me. That's the kind of tone!"

"Well, go on then. Why did you feel that you had to hide the tone from me?"

"Oh my God, I didn't want to frighten you! I was hoping it would all settle down on its own. But soon after my father returned we had dinner together. I was fully prepared to respond to each of his demands, clearly, solidly and seriously, but it didn't quite work out that way. He never even brought up the subject! He's very clever. Instead, he behaved like there was nothing to talk about, as if the whole matter was settled and there couldn't possibly be any room for discussion. Not even a chance to discuss it! Can you believe such arrogance? And then he became so friendly and affectionate toward me, I was shocked. Oh, yes, he's a very clever man, my father, if you only knew. He reads everything and knows everything. He only has to look at you once and he can read your every thought. Maybe that's why he's been called a Jesuit. Natasha doesn't like it when I praise him. Please don't be mad at me, Natasha. And another thing: he never used to give me money, but yesterday he did! Natasha, my angel, our money worries are over. Here, look! Everything he held back when he was punishing me, a full six months' allowance, he's made up for!"

He took from his pocket a huge bundle of fifteen hundred rubles and tossed it on the table.

"Look how much!" he said. "I haven't counted it yet. So you see, Mavra, you won't need to pawn any more spoons or cuff-links for us!"

Mavra looked surprised and delighted by this news and regarded Alyosha with newfound respect.

Natasha urged him to continue his story. "Well," he said, "what am I going to do now? How can I go against his wishes? I swear to you both that if he had come out and given me orders, I would have stood up to him like a man and refused him. But now, what can I say? I can see you're unhappy with me, Natasha. From the way you two are looking at each other, I can see you think I've been trod upon and there is not an ounce of strength in me. There is strength in me and it's even more than you think. And to prove it, I said to myself 'I have a duty to my father and I should tell him everything.' So I did. I expressed myself and he listened."

"Yes, well, what exactly did you express to him?" Natasha asked with a sense of foreboding.

"That I do not want another fiancée, that I already have a fiancée, and it is you. I didn't exactly say it in those words, but I was preparing him and I plan to tell him tomorrow. So I've solved that problem. But what I did tell him is that marrying for money is shameful and ignoble and that it was silly for us to consider ourselves aristocrats. I was very frank with him, you see, and spoke to him man to man. There are different levels of aristocracy, I said, and using his own measuring standards, we are no different from anyone else, and I am proud to be like everyone else. I spoke with great fire and passion. I even surprised myself. I proved to him, from his point of view, that we are princes in name only. First of all, I said, 'What makes a prince? Wealth. Wealth is the main thing, the principal thing that makes a prince. Nowadays, Rothschild is a prince among princes.' Then I said, 'A prince's place in society is also essential. High society has forgotten about our family long ago, they rarely think about us today.' Uncle Semyon was renowned in Moscow for having frivolously squandered away his estate and more than 300 serfs, and my father might well have been forced to become a ploughman, like so many other princes, had he not married my mother. So I proved to him, clearly and eloquently, that there really is no reputation for us to maintain. He never objected to anything I said, but he did suggest that I continue to call on Count Nainsky to keep in good with him, and that I must be pleasant to Princess K., my godmother, because she has influence in the world and can introduce me to the proper people. I tell you all this, Natasha, to show you just how much I gave up when I fell in love with you; such was the effect of your influence. Until now, my father has avoided speaking about you directly. He and I are both cunning, waiting for the right moment to spring, and you can be sure there is great sport to be had when that happens!"

"Yes, but enough of that. What was the result? Is anything resolved? That's the important thing, Alyosha. You do prattle on so!"

"Oh, good Lord, Natasha, it's impossible to know what he's decided. As for my prattling, it's not true. I don't prattle. Father hasn't decided upon anything, but he did listen to all of my arguments and he smiled at me, as if he pitied me, which may not be the ideal response, but it shows he cares. And he did say, 'I understand and I quite agree with you.' Then he added, 'When we go to Count Nainsky's home it may be best to say nothing about this, as they may not understand as well as I do.' It seems they don't entirely understand him either, because they're angry with him about something. I don't think they like him very much. When I first went there, the count was very arrogant and condescending to me; as if he had totally forgotten that I had grown up in his household. I think he was angry at me because of my ingratitude, but really there is no ingratitude whatever. It's just so boring in his house, so I stopped visiting.

"The count has treated my father very cavalierly too; so haughty and proud, in fact, that it's a wonder my father continues to go there. I know he only puts up with them for my benefit, but I never asked him too. I thought about confronting my father about the count but I held my tongue; I knew it would only make him angrier. So I came up with a plan that was quite ingenious. I determined to make the count respect me and like me. And I succeeded perfectly. Everything changed in a single day."

"Listen, Alyosha," Natasha interrupted. "I thought you were going to tell me something that concerned *us*. I don't care about how you ingratiated yourself to the count. I couldn't care less about the count."

"Couldn't care less? Do you hear her, Ivan Petrovich? She says she couldn't care less. The count is the most important part of my story and you will care when you hear the rest. Just let me finish. The two of you, let's be honest, often treat me like a fool. Well, maybe I do say or do foolish things on occasion, but I can be very clever when I want to be and this is one of those times. When you hear what I've done, I know you will both agree that I'm not at all stupid."

"That's silly, my darling, no one considers you stupid." Natasha refused to accept the idea that Alyosha might be a little slow-witted, and on those occasions when I pointed out this fact, she became very angry with me. She hated to see him humiliated in any way. Although she was certainly aware of his limitations, she never gave a hint of her feelings to him for fear of hurting his pride. Alyosha, however, was acutely sensitive to such insults and always knew what Natasha was thinking. Natasha would then try to placate him with excessive flattery and soothing words. That is why Alyosha's current rant was creating conflicting emotions in her heart. "You shouldn't put yourself down like that, Alyosha. You're just a little frivolous, that's all."

"Exactly," he responded. "So I'll prove to you I know what I am doing. After the reception at the count's, I knew father was angry with me, but I thought to myself, 'Hold off, don't say anything yet.' Then we went to visit the princess. I had heard that she was quite old and senile and almost completely deaf, but that she loves dogs. She has a whole flock and adores them all. In spite of her frailties, she has such an enormous influence in society that even a proud man like the count bows down to her. Isn't that a charming image? So during the carriage ride with my father, I came up with a plan of action, and what do you think I based it on? Simply the fact that dogs *love* me! I don't know why, but I seem to have a magnetic attraction to them, or maybe it's just because I love all animals so much. Oh, Natasha, speaking of magnetic attractions, we had a séance the other day. It's terribly interesting, Ivan Petrovich. Amazing! I called up Julius Caesar."

"Oh, my God, why would you want to speak to Julius Caesar?" Natasha cried. She was once again convulsed by laughter. "That's all that was missing!"

"Yes, well I... Wait, why shouldn't I want to speak to Julius Caesar? I don't see what's so funny?"

"Nothing, nothing," she said, trying to resume her serious demeanor. "What did Julius Caesar have to say to you?"

"Well, he didn't say anything to me," he responded, looking quite offended by the suggestion. "I simply held a pencil and he moved it around on the paper. At least, they said it was Julius Caesar doing the writing, but, of course, I'm not sure I believed them."

"Well then, what did Julius Caesar write?" Natasha asked.

"I couldn't tell. It ended up looking something like 'moisten it,' like in Gogol. Completely illegible."

Growing more frustrated, Natasha prompted him, "Yes, well, tell us about the princess now."

"Well, you keep interrupting me! We arrived at the princess's home and I began flirting immediately with Mimi. Mimi is the nastiest, most contemptible and obstinate little dog, and a biter, but the princess is crazy about her. I think they may be the same age. I started by giving candy to Mimi and within ten minutes, she learned how to give me her paw, something she had never done before in her entire life! The princess was absolutely thrilled and almost crying from happiness. 'Oh, Mimi," she cries, 'you gave me your paw, you gave me your paw.' Then someone walked in the room and she said, 'Mimi, give him your paw!' and Mimi did so and she cried, 'Oh, she shook your hand! She shook your hand! My godson taught her that trick!' And then the count came in and the princess said, 'Mimi can shake hands!' and she looked at me with such tender emotion; she's really a very sweet old lady, I almost pity her. Well, then I needed to come up with something else to do. Fortunately, she dropped her snuff box. I saw immediately that there was a portrait painted on it of her as a bride sixty years ago, so I pretended I didn't know it was her and said, "What a charming picture, this is an ideal beauty!" Well, the princess just melted completely. She asked me about this and about that, and where had I studied, and who do I visit, and told me what glorious hair I have, and it was all so boring and predictable, but she absolutely adores me. I made her laugh by telling her a risqué story. She loves that sort of thing. Of course, she shook her bony old finger at me, but laughed anyway. When she finally permitted me to leave, she kissed me and blessed me and made me promise to come every day to entertain her. The count took my hand and his eyes oozed steel. My father, one of the most noble and honest of human beings, whether you believe it or not, nearly cried from happiness during our carriage ride, and when we arrived at his home he embraced me and became mysteriously frank and open about my career, connections, money, marriages. I couldn't follow most of what he had to say, but that's when he gave me the money. That was yesterday. Tomorrow I'm going to see the princess again, but don't ever doubt that my father is an honorable man, even if he does want me to break up with you. He's just blinded by the millions that Katya has and you don't. He wants them for me and it's just his ignorance that makes him behave unjustly towards you. What father doesn't want happiness for his son? It's not his fault that he thinks money and happiness go hand in hand. They all think like that. But when you see things from his standpoint, you can easily see that he's right. I hurried over here immediately to assure you that any prejudices you may have against him are unfounded since he is, it goes without saying, completely innocent. I don't blame you at all."

"So all that's really happened is that you've set yourself up with the princess. Is that the cunning plan you spoke of?" Natasha asked.

"What? No. What are you saying? That's just the beginning. I only told you about the princess so you could see how I plan to control my father. But that part of the story hasn't started yet."

"Well, say something," Natasha pleaded.

"Today, something else happened that was so extraordinary that I am still astonished by it. I've already mentioned that my father and the countess have been playing matchmaker, but until now there's been no official announcement, so it's not too late to break it off without creating a scandal. Count Nainsky is the only other person who knows and he is, after all, a relative and patron. And even though Katya and I have grown very close over the past two weeks, we have never said a word about the future. Or of marriage. Or even love. Before anything like that could happen, we would need to obtain the consent of Princess K., from whom all good fortune and influence flow. If she approves, the world will approve, that's how influential she is. And the countess, Katya's stepmother, is very anxious for me to be accepted into society. It's very important to her. You see, her reputation abroad has followed her home and the princess absolutely refuses to receive her. That's why the countess has changed her mind about me. She thinks that my marriage to Katya would be her entrée into society, so she was particularly delighted by my success with the princess. But none of that is important. The main thing is that even though I've known Katerina Fedorovna most of my life, even last year I was still just a boy and didn't know anything about women. So I never thought much about her."

"The fact is that you were in love with me a year ago," interrupted Natasha. "That's why you didn't think about her, but now..."

"Not another word, Natasha!" Alyosha exclaimed hotly. "You are mistaken and you wound me! I won't bother to contradict you, but you should listen and you'll learn everything! Oh, if you only knew Katya, what a tender, gentle and open-hearted creature she is.

But listen and you'll know everything. Two weeks ago, when my father took me to see Katya, I decided to study her very closely. And then I noticed that she was studying me closely too. Well, of course, that aroused my curiosity, and her interest in me, combined with my father's letter, prompted me to double my efforts to get to know her better. I'm not going to shower you with her praises but I will say one thing. She is the one bright exception to her whole dreary circle. She has such a strong, straightforward spirit and a pure and honest soul that she makes me feel like a little boy in her presence, like a little brother, despite the fact that she is only seventeen years old.

"I also noticed," he continued, "that there is something secretly melancholy about her. She rarely says anything when she's at home and seems intimidated and frightened about something. She's clearly afraid of my father and has no love for her stepmother, although for some reason the countess pretends Katya just adores her, which isn't true. Katya obeys her, of course, but nothing more. So four days ago, after all my observations, I decided to proceed with my plan, which I successfully carried out today. And that was to tell Katya everything, confess the truth, and get her on our side once and for all."

"What do you mean?" Natasha asked uneasily. "What is there to tell her, what is there to confess?"

"Everything. Absolutely everything," Alyosha responded. "And I thank God for inspiring me to do it, but listen to the rest. Listen. Four days ago I decided to stay away from you until I had brought this business to an end. I knew that if I were with you, I would just follow your advice and never be able to build up my strength and resolve. So that's what I did and I was brave and I did precisely what I set out to do, which was to come back to you with a solution. And I have."

"Well, what is it? Tell us faster!"

"It's very simple! I approached her boldly and honestly and... but wait. Before that I need to tell you one other thing that surprised me very much. My father received a letter this morning. I was about to enter his office and saw him standing there staring at this letter and he seemed quite surprised by its contents. At first, he said nothing, but then he started to smile and move about excitedly, and then he was laughing like a madman. I was afraid to enter the room until he calmed down. When I did go in, he spoke to me in a vague, hazy sort of way and told me to be quick and prepare for a visit to Katya. I thought it was pretty early in the day for a visit, but I did as I was told. You know, Natasha, you must have been misinformed about there being a party there today because there was no one else there."

"Oh, Alyosha, don't be distracted. Just tell me, please, what did you say to Katya?"

"Well, fortunately, we had two full hours to ourselves. I simply told her that in spite of any plans being made for us to marry, it wasn't going to happen, and that in my heart I felt great sympathy for her, but she was the only one who could save me. Then I told her everything. Can you believe it, Natasha? She knew absolutely nothing about you and me. If only you could have seen how touched she was by our story. At first, she turned pale and seemed a little frightened. But when I told her how you had run away from your home, and how we had been living, and how we had suffered, and that we were now coming to her for help—told her I was speaking for you too, Natasha—and that we needed her to intercede for us by going to her stepmother and telling her that she refused to marry me. That was our only hope I told her and only she could rescue us. Katya listened with such sweet, sympathetic eyes. You can't imagine how lovely her eyes looked at that moment. I think her entire soul passed through those sparkling, blue eyes. She thanked me for being honest with her and promised to help us. Then she started asking questions about you and told me she wanted to meet you and get to know you, and that she wanted you to know that she already loved you like a sister and she hoped you would love *her* like a sister. Then when I told her I hadn't seen you in five days, she chased me away and insisted I go directly to you."

Natasha was touched. "And you wasted so much time telling us about some old princess and her nasty dog, when you had this to reveal? Oh, Alyosha, Alyosha," Natasha said reproachfully. "How did Katya behave when she released you? Was she pleased and happy or did it seem unimportant to her?"

"Yes, she was very pleased that she could act in so noble a manner, but she cried nevertheless, because she loves me too, Natasha. She admitted that she's come to love me; that she doesn't see anyone else, and that she has liked me for a long time. She was especially attracted to me because she is surrounded by craftiness and lies. Compared to the others, I am sincere and honest. Then she stood up and started to say, 'God be with you, Alexey Petrovich, I wish you…' but before she could finish, she burst into tears and ran out of the room. We did agree, however, that she will talk to her stepmother tomorrow and tell her that she won't marry me, and I'm to have an equally serious conversation with my father informing him of our decision. She criticized me for not having told him before and said, 'An honest person has nothing to fear.'

"She is so noble," Alyosha continued. "She doesn't like my father because she thinks he is too devious and money-hungry. I tried to defend him, but she didn't believe me. She said if I can't convince him to call off the wedding—and she doesn't think I'll succeed—then I will have to resort to the patronage of Princess K., because my father wouldn't dare go against her wishes. We both gave each other our word to be like brother and sister. Oh, Natasha, if only you knew her history and how unhappy she is living with the countess and her friends. She hates them all. Of course, she didn't tell me that directly, but I could see what was in her heart. She would love you so much, Natasha, and once you saw what a good heart she has, you would feel the same way about her. You two were born to be sisters. I was thinking that I'd like to get you two together and then just stand back and admire you both. I hope you don't mind my talking about her like this, Natasha. I wouldn't want you to misunderstand. I love talking about her to you and about you to her. You know very well that I love you more than anyone, you're my all!"

Natasha looked silently at him. There was great affection in her eyes but sadness too, somehow. It was as if his words had both caressed and tortured her at the same time.

"I started to admire Katya more than two weeks ago," Alyosha said. "I would drive there every night and then come home and think of the two of you, comparing each of your qualities."

"And who came out on top?" Natasha asked with a smile.

"Sometimes you and sometimes her, but you always won out in the end. Whenever I speak with her, I always feel so much better about myself afterwards, more clever and manly and noble. Well, tomorrow all will be decided."

"Don't you feel a little sorry for her, Alyosha? You said she loves you; you noticed that yourself."

"Yes, of course, I feel sorry. But the three of us shall love each other and then..."

"And then good-bye," Natasha said quietly, almost to herself.

Alyosha looked puzzled by this remark, but before he could comment, the conversation was interrupted in a most unexpected manner. There was a sudden noise in the kitchen, which also served as the entryway to the apartment. Mavra poked her head in the doorway and beckoned to Alyosha.

"There is someone asking for you," Mavra said in a mysterious whisper.

"Who could be asking about me *here*?" Alyosha said, turning to us with a bewildered look. "I'll go see."

In the kitchen stood Prince Valkovsky's uniformed valet. The prince had been passing Natasha's building in his carriage and stopped to inquire if Alyosha was there with her. After speaking with Alyosha, the valet left.

"That's very odd," Alyosha said, looking very confused. "He's never done that before."

Natasha too looked most uneasy.

Suddenly the door opened again and Mavra hurried in. "The prince is coming up," she whispered, then ducked out again.

Natasha turned pale and stood up. Suddenly, her eyes caught fire and she leaned against the table as she stared at the door through which her uninvited guest was about to appear.

"Natasha, don't be frightened, I'm with you. I won't let him bully you," Alyosha said, attempting to suppress any fear that he may have been feeling.

The door opened and on the threshold stood Prince Valkovsky, in person.

CHAPTER SEVENTEEN

As Valkovsky's steely glance darted quickly around the room, taking in each of us, I found it difficult to determine his attitude—was he enemy or friend? I'll take a moment to provide a more detailed description of his appearance.

I had seen him before when I was a boy. Now he was a man of about 45, no more, with strong, extremely attractive features. His expression could change instantly, depending on the circumstances, from pleasant charm to sullen anger. His ideally formed oval face featured a dark complexion that set off his excellent teeth, small, thin lips, straight but slightly hooked nose, broad, wrinkle-free forehead and suitably large, gray eyes, the totality of which represented a handsome man but, nevertheless, did not elicit an agreeable response. One always had the sensation that his expression was a facade, deliberately created, borrowed from others for a particular purpose, and that you were not seeing his true feelings. If you studied him more intently, however, you would begin to notice something malicious, devious and decidedly selfish behind the mask. What drew your attention most prominently were his gray eyes. They seemed to have a will of their own. When he wanted to gaze gently and affectionately, his eyes would often reflect a rigid, distrustful and even malevolent ray. The rest of him was decidedly elegant. He was reasonably thin, with soft, dark brown hair which had yet to turn gray, giving him an appearance younger than his actual years. His ears, hands and feet were also remarkably good. He was, in total, a thoroughbred. His one lapse may have been his sense of fashion, which tended to favor the styles of much younger men. He seemed more like a big brother to Alyosha, making it difficult for a stranger to accept him as the father of an adult son.

Valkovsky approached Natasha directly and said to her, "My arrival at your home at this hour without advance notice is certainly unusual and outside the rules of proper etiquette, but I hope you will believe that I am, at least, fully aware of the eccentricity of my behavior. I also understand with whom I am dealing. I know that you are an insightful and generous woman. If you will permit me just ten minutes of your time, I believe I will be able to justify my surprise visit."

He said all of this politely, but with an air of forceful determination.

"Won't you sit?" said Natasha, who had not yet fully recovered from her initial surprise and fright.

The prince bowed and sat down.

"First of all, permit me to say a few words to you," he said, indicating his son. "Alyosha, you left earlier without waiting for me and without even saying good-bye to the countess or providing any excuse for your behavior. Shortly after you rushed out, we were informed that Katerina Fedorovna had fainted. The countess was about to go to her when Katya hurried in on her own. She told us straight out that she cannot be your wife and intended to join a convent. She said that you had asked for her help by acknowledging that you were in love with another woman, Natalia Nikolayevna. Katya was clearly devastated by this information and her announcement, it goes without saying, was completely unexpected and both surprised and frightened me. Traveling past your house just now, I noticed a light in your window," he continued, turning to Natasha. "An idea which I have been considering for some time took hold of me and I felt a strong determination to convey it to you. You will, I hope, excuse the sharp manner in which I express myself, but this has come upon me so suddenly..."

"I'm sure that I will consider whatever you have to say," Natasha said hesitatingly.

The prince stared intently into her eyes, perhaps trying to read her thoughts.

"I look forward to your insight," he continued, "and hope you understand that even though I may have arrived here unexpectedly, I understand precisely with whom I am dealing. We have known each other a long time and I realize that my behavior towards you in the past may have appeared very troubling and unjust. But you are aware of the unpleasantness that exists between your father and me. I don't try to justify myself. Perhaps I am more to blame than I realized until recently. If that's true, it's because I was deceived by information that was presented to me. I often leap to negative conclusions, I admit. I tend to suspect the worst before seeing the best, an unfortunate characteristic of a bitter heart. But I don't try to hide my faults. I believed the rumors about you, and when you ran off with Alyosha I was very worried about him. But I didn't really know you at the time. The information that I have since gathered about you, little by little, comforted me and as I continued to observe Alyosha's behavior, I grew more and more encouraged until finally I realized that my suspicions about you were groundless. I learned that you had thrown off your ties with your parents and that your father was dead set against you marrying my son. I also realized that you were not using your influence over Alyosha to coerce him into marriage. That fact alone clearly demonstrated that you are an admirable young woman."

The prince bowed his head courteously to Natasha.

"Nevertheless," he continued, "I fully admit that I have used every power within my means to prevent any possibility of your marrying my son. I know I may be expressing myself too bluntly, but I believe that it's important for me to be brutally honest with you and hope that you will listen, understand, and agree with me. Shortly after you left your home, I left St. Petersburg, but I was no longer afraid for Alyosha's well-being. I knew that your pride would not permit you to marry him until after our family troubles had ended, nor would you stand between Alyosha and his obligations to me, knowing that I would never forgive him for marrying you. You also didn't want it said about you that you had set your sights on finding the son of a prince for a fiancé just so you could enter into his family. On the contrary, you showed very little interest in us and may well have been waiting for me to approach you to request the honor of your marrying my son. But whatever the circumstances, I continued to be your enemy. I'm not trying to justify my behavior, but I will provide you with an explanation. It's really very simple. You are unknown in society and you are not rich. Although I do have some money, our family name is on the decline. Money and connections are very important to us. The countess's stepdaughter has no connections, but she is very rich. If we delay much longer, there are bound to be other suitors and Katya will find another bridegroom. It's very important that that not happen, and although Alyosha is still very young, I am determined that he shall marry Katya. You see, I am very honest with you, I'm hiding nothing.

"You may well look with contempt upon a father who admits to pushing his son into marriage solely for his own self-interest and enhancement. It's certainly a reprehensible act to expect the son to cast aside a wonderful girl who has sacrificed everything for him. But I make no apologies. There is a second reason why I want my son to marry the stepdaughter of Countess Zinaida Filimonova. Katya is a girl worthy of the highest respect and love. She has been beautifully brought up, has a sweet and gentle nature and is very bright, although in some respects still a child. Alyosha has none of these qualities. He is frivolous, obstinate and, at twenty-two, still a complete child. He has, perhaps, one positive virtue, a good heart, but even that can be a dangerous attribute when combined with his other deficiencies. I realized a long time ago that my influence over him is on the decline. His youthful enthusiasm has pushed aside his sense of responsibility. I'm very fond of the boy, but there is very little I can do to control him. But it's important for him to be under the influence of someone with a high moral character. Alyosha has a weak and submissive nature and is easily influenced by others. It's far simpler for him to be loved and controlled by someone else than to try to be a leader himself. He'll be that way the rest of his life. So you can imagine how delighted I was to discover in Katerina Fedorovna the ideal wife for my son. But that delight soon vanished when I realized that there was an even greater influence exerting its pull on Alyosha. And that's you. When I returned to St. Petersburg, I noticed a remarkable change in Alyosha. True, he was still childish and flighty, but I saw some nobler qualities emerging. He thought less about toys and more about honor and higher aspirations, for example. Some of his ideas were rather strange and unsound, of course, sometimes even absurd, but his inclinations and desires were better and stronger. He seemed to be building upon a stronger foundation and I credit that change entirely to you," the prince said, nodding his head toward Natasha. "You have, in a sense, re-educated him. I acknowledge that. There was, in fact, a moment when I thought that you might actually be the right woman to make Alyosha happy. But I quickly pushed that idea out of my head. I needed to find a way to distract him away from you at any cost. So I put my plan into action and I thought I was close to achieving my goal. Until an hour ago, I thought victory was mine. But then that incident at the countess's house cast aside all those assumptions, and the simple fact occurred to me that Alyosha is truly serious about his attachment to you. Moreover, the tenacity and strength of that attachment is remarkable. I say it again, you have re-educated him, and the degree to which you have accomplished that task is greater even than I had imagined.

"Today he demonstrated to me an intelligence which I had, by no means, suspected, and at the same time a remarkable grace and level-headedness. He chose the most efficient route possible to maneuver himself out of a difficult situation. He accomplished this by appealing to the noblest instincts of the human heart, the ability to pardon and repay an unkind act with generosity. He went to the very person creating the obstruction and requested her involvement and assistance. He instilled pride in a woman who already loved him while at the same time admitting that she had a rival, by creating sympathy for that rival by a promise of sisterly friendship. To attain his goal without insult or offense is something not even the most adroit of wise men could accomplish, but only someone with a fresh, unblemished and focused heart. I am confident that you, Natalia Nikolayevna, had no hand in Alyosha's act today either by suggestion or advice. In fact, you've probably just learned about it from him a little while ago, if I'm not mistaken. Am I?"

"No, you're not mistaken," Natasha answered. Her entire face and eyes glowed with a lustrous light, much like that of inspiration. The prince's words were already having an effect on her. "I haven't seen Alyosha in five days," she added. "He thought of it and carried it out all by himself."

"That may be true," the prince said, "but clearly this unexpected ingenuity, this determination, this noble fortitude, are all the result of your influence on him. I came to that realization during my ride here and, as a result of that, have come to a decision. My matchmaking plans with the countess have been irreparably destroyed, but if it's not to be, it's not to be. But I have determined that you alone can make Alyosha happy and serve as his guide. In fact, you've already set off on the road to his future happiness. I've kept nothing from you and I'm not hiding anything from you now. I make no secret of my love for money, connections, nobility, even rank. I know this is prejudice, but I love my prejudices and it's difficult to cast them aside. But there are circumstances when other considerations must take precedence. For one thing, I love my son, and I've reached the conclusion that he must either remain with you or perish without you. I admit that I probably reached that conclusion a month ago, but it's only today that I can fully acknowledge it. I could have visited you tomorrow to tell you all this, instead of imposing on you at this late hour, but perhaps my eagerness to speak to you tonight will convince you of my passion and sincerity. I'm not a child. I certainly wouldn't rush to make such an important decision without considering all sides of the issue. When I entered your home this evening I was already resolved, but I feel it may take a while before I can satisfactorily convince you of my sincerity. But on to the business at hand! Let me tell you why I came here. I came to offer you my sincerest gratitude and most solemn respect, and to ask you, please, to do me the honor of accepting my son's hand in marriage. Do not think that I stand here as a terrible father who has finally decided to forgive his children and graciously agree to their happiness. No, no, you would be giving me too much credit by assuming me capable of such sentiments. Nor should you think that I came here confident of your answer, knowing how much you have sacrificed for him. Again no! I'll be the first to admit that he doesn't deserve you. He's a good boy and he himself can confirm this, but that is insignificant. I came here to beg you," he said, standing with a great show of solemnity and respect, "to accept me as your friend. I know I have no right to expect this of you, but please give me some hope that you will allow me to earn that right. May I hope?"

The prince bowed respectfully and awaited Natasha's reply.

The whole time he had been speaking, I had been watching him carefully. He was aware of this.

I later realized that his speech had been quite inconsistent in a number of respects. His tone did not, at first, correspond to the alleged impulse that drew him to us at that awkward hour. Some of his comments seemed noticeably rehearsed and in other places he seemed to be affecting an artificial joviality to hide his feelings with careless humor and jokes. These thoughts occurred to me later, but my perception at the time was quite different. His final words were conveyed with such emotion and sincere respect for Natasha, and the sparkle of teardrops on his eyelashes was so convincing, that he easily conquered Natasha's noble heart. She, like him, rose and stood silently before him for a moment. Then she raised her hand and extended it to him. The prince accepted her hand and kissed it tenderly. Alyosha reacted enthusiastically.

"Didn't I tell you, Natasha?" he said with great excitement. "You didn't believe me! You wouldn't believe me when I told you that he was the noblest person in the world! But now you can see for yourself!" Alyosha rushed to his father and embraced him warmly. Valkovsky returned his embrace but hurriedly pulled away, clearly embarrassed to express his feelings openly.

"Enough," he said, picking up his hat, "I have to go. I asked for ten minutes of your time and have taken a full hour. Before I go, however, I would like to ask if you will permit me to call again as soon as possible, and as often as possible?"

"Yes, yes!" Natasha answered, "As often as possible. I would like to learn how to love you," she added with some confusion.

"You are so straight-forward, so honest!" the prince said, smiling at her. "You refuse to be insincere even out of courtesy. I like that. It's so much more refreshing than the false politeness of most of the people I know. Yes, I realize more than ever how hard I will have to work to deserve your love!"

"Please, you flatter me too much!" she said shyly, looking especially endearing at that moment.

"As you wish," Valkovsky said, "but permit me two additional words. Regrettably, I am unable to visit you tomorrow or the day after. I received a letter today that demands my immediate attention. I leave tomorrow morning. But I wouldn't want you to think that I stopped in this evening merely because I was unavailable tomorrow or the next day. I know you'd never think of such a thing, but I am overly concerned about such matters. It's my suspicious nature; the same suspicious nature that has caused so many problems in my life and resulted in the unfortunate misunderstanding with your father. Let's see. Today is Tuesday. Wednesday, Thursday and Friday I shall be away from St. Petersburg, returning on Saturday. Without fail, I shall visit you on Saturday. May I count on your company for the entire evening?"

"Without fail, without fail!" Natasha was almost giddy with excitement. "I'll expect you on Saturday evening. I can't wait!"

"You make me very happy," Valkovsky said. "I look forward to getting to know you better." He turned suddenly to me and extended his hand. "But I can't leave without taking a moment to shake your hand. I hope you will excuse the informal nature of our conversation. I know we've met before and have even been formally introduced, but I'd like to tell you how pleasant it is to renew your acquaintance."

"Yes, we have met before," I said, "but I honestly can't recall our having been introduced."

"It was at Prince Rudolph's, last year."

"Oh, I'm sorry, I had forgotten," I said. "But I promise you that this time I will not forget. This evening will be especially memorable."

"Yes, to me also. I have known for some time what a sincere, honest friend you have been to Natalia Nikolayevna and my son. I hope you will permit me to be a fourth to your threesome. Is that possible?" he added, turning to Natasha.

"Yes, Vanya has been our dear friend, and I would love it if we could all be together," she said.

Poor Natasha. She was glowing with happiness when she saw the prince engage me in conversation. She loved me!

"I've met many people who admire your talent," the prince continued. "I know in particular two such worshippers who would be delighted to meet you. They are my dear friend, the countess, and her stepdaughter, Katerina Fedorovna. I trust you will not refuse me the pleasure of presenting you to these two ladies."

"I'm flattered and would be delighted to meet them. I know so few people."

"Well, give me your address. Where do you live? It would be a pleasure to..."

"I really don't receive visitors, Prince, at least not at present."

"Of course, I wouldn't presume to make myself an exception, but..."

"No, please, you're most welcome to stop in, if you'd like. I live in an alley off Voznesensky Prospect in Klugen's building."

"Klugen's building!" he exclaimed, as if startled by the news. "When... Have you lived their long?"

"No, just a short time," I answered, aware that he was scrutinizing me closely. "I live in apartment forty-four."

"Forty-four? Do you live alone?"

"Yes, quite alone."

"Ah, yes... then... It seems I know this house. So much better. I will, without fail, visit you. I have so much to tell you and I expect to hear a great deal from you. You, in a great many ways, can be of assistance to me. But, you see, I begin by asking you a favor. Before I've even visited! Again, your hand!"

He shook my hand and Alyosha's, then kissed Natasha's, and left, without asking Alyosha to follow him.

The three of us were very confused. All of this had happened so unexpectedly that we were quite unprepared. It seemed to each of us that a great deal had changed, in one moment, and that we were on the brink of something new and unknown.

Alyosha squatted next to Natasha and quietly kissed her hands. He barely looked at her, perhaps afraid of what she might say.

"Alyosha, my dear," she said at last, "I want you to go to Katarina Fedorovna tomorrow."

"I was just thinking that myself," he said. "I'll go."

"But it might be difficult for her to see you. What should we do?"

"I don't know, my darling, I was thinking that too. Let me think on it. I'll see... I'll figure out something." Unable to restrain his excitement, Alyosha added, "Everything has certainly changed for us now, Natasha!"

She smiled and looked at him tenderly.

"And how diplomatic he was," Alyosha said to me. "He knew about your poor apartment and said nothing."

"Nothing of what?" I asked.

"Well... of your moving... or anything," he said, his cheeks turning red.

"That's ridiculous, Alyosha, why should he have said anything?" I asked.

"Well, that's what I'm saying. He was very discreet. But he did praise you! I told you he would... I told you. He's very understanding and caring. But he treated me like a child. They all do. But, in a way, I guess I really am."

"You are a child," Natasha said, "but you're more perceptive than all of us. You're a good person, Alyosha."

"But he said that my good heart would get me in trouble. What did he mean? I don't understand. But, Natasha, shouldn't I hurry after him? I can come see you in the morning."

"Yes, go my darling, that's a good idea. Go see him immediately, do you hear? But come back tomorrow as early as possible. You're not going to disappear for another five days, are you?" she added slyly, caressing him with her eyes.

We were all feeling a quiet, complete contentment.

"Are you coming with me, Vanya?" Alyosha shouted as he left the room.

"No, he'll stay with me a little longer. I have something else to say to Vanya. But be here early tomorrow."

"First thing! Goodnight, Mavra."

Mavra was very excited. She had listened to the prince's speech, had overheard everything, but she didn't understand it all. She could guess some of it but wanted to question us about the rest. But meanwhile, she looked very serious, even proud. She too realized that much had changed.

At last we were alone. Natasha took my hand but remained silent for a while, as if searching for the words.

"I'm tired," she said finally in a weak voice. "Listen, are you going to see *them* tomorrow?"

"Of course."

"Tell Mama, but don't tell him."

"Yes. I never speak to him about you."

"Well, he'll hear about it anyway. But pay attention to what he says, his state of mind. My God, Vanya, would he really curse me for this marriage? No, he couldn't."

"The prince will have to fix this," I said hurriedly. "He'll have to reconcile with them, and then everything will be settled."

"Oh my God, I hope that happens. I pray it happens."

"Don't worry, Natasha, it'll happen. All signs point to it."

She stared at me a moment.

"What do you think of the prince?"

"Well, if he meant what he said, then, in my opinion, he is a very decent man."

"If he meant what he said? What do you mean by that? He couldn't possibly have been deceiving us!"

"I'm sure you're right," I answered. Then a thought flashed through my mind. "It was strange."

"You were staring at him so intently."

"Yes, there was something strange about him, it seems to me."

"I thought so too. He said so many things... Oh, my dear Vanya, I'm tired. You should be going. But tomorrow, come see me as early as possible after seeing them. And one last thing. You don't think I was insulting when I said I'd like to learn how to love him, do you?"

"No, why insulting?"

"Or foolish? It seemed like I was saying that I didn't like him now."

"Quite the opposite. It was wonderful, and sweet, and spontaneous. You looked so wonderful at that moment. If he didn't understand that, then he's a fool."

"I thought you looked angry at me, Vanya. That's wrong of me. I'm very suspicious and vain. Now don't laugh at me. I never hide anything from you. Ah, Vanya, you are my dearest friend, my guide. If ever I'm unhappy, I know you'll always be there to comfort me. You may even be the only one. What can I ever do to repay you? Don't ever curse me, Vanya!"

As soon as I got home I undressed and got into bed. My room was as dark and damp as a cellar. Many strange thoughts and sensations were crowding my mind and it was a long time before I could fall asleep.

But there was one man who was probably laughing at us that very minute as he lay in his comfortable bed, if he even thought of us at all. Which I doubted.

CHAPTER EIGHTEEN

At 10 o'clock the next morning, I was rushing out of my apartment to visit the Ichmenyevs on Vasilyevsky Island, to be followed by a visit to Natasha, when I ran into my tiny visitor from the previous evening, Jeremiah Smith's granddaughter. I don't know why, but I was delighted to see her. It had been impossible to get a good look at her in the shadows of dusk, but in the morning light I was even more astonished by her appearance. It would be difficult to imagine a stranger, more unique creature.

Small, with large, black, non-Russian eyes and long, thick and tangled black hair, her silent and mysterious stare would have attracted the attention of anyone in the street. Indeed, the most striking aspect of her face was the perpetual gaze of mistrust, even suspicion.

Her tattered and filthy dress looked more like a pile of discarded rags in the daylight. She seemed to me the victim of some slow, lingering and fatal illness that was gradually sapping the life out of her. Her thin face was deathly pale with a yellowish tint, but in spite of her fading health, the dirt and the rags, she had a haunting kind of beauty. Her eyebrows were sharp, thin and very beautiful, her broad, low forehead was unusually striking, and her lips, although nearly colorless, were perfectly formed and suggested a bold and proud character.

"Oh, you're here again," I said. "I had a feeling you'd show up again."

She stepped into the room slowly and cautiously, just as she had the night before, and looked around. She seemed to be inspecting each detail of the room, as if taking inventory of each of the changes that had occurred since her grandfather had lived here. "Like grandfather, like granddaughter," I thought. For a moment, I worried that she might be insane. She stood silently for the longest time.

"The books," she whispered finally, staring at the floor.

"Yes, your books, I have them. I was holding onto them for you."

She looked at me curiously and I recognized a hint of a smile, but she caught herself and returned to her former haughty and mysterious expression.

"Did Grandpa mention me to you?" she asked, surveying me from head to toe.

"No, he didn't, but he..."

"Then how did you know that I would show up again?" she asked sharply. "Who told you?"

"Because it seemed to me that your grandfather couldn't have lived all alone, without help. He was very old, weak, and I thought there must be someone who looked in on him. Here are your books. Are you learning from them?"

"No."

"Then why do you have them?"

"Grandpa taught me out of them when I used to visit."

"Then why did you stop visiting?"

"I didn't. I got sick," she offered as an excuse.

"What family do you have? A father and a mother?"

She lowered her eyebrows and frowned at me with a scared look in her eyes. Suddenly and quietly, she turned and headed for the door just as she had the night before. I followed her with my eyes, but she stopped on the threshold.

Turning slightly toward me, as she had when she asked about Azorka, she asked, "What did he die of?"

I went to her and began to recount the incidents leading up to her grandfather's death. She listened quietly but carefully, her back still towards me. I mentioned that her grandfather had spoken about the Sixth Line just before his death. I had assumed that someone near to him lived there and that they would come to inquire about him.

"He must have loved you very much," I said, "to think of you at the moment of his death."

"No," she said, almost involuntarily. "He didn't love me."

She was clearly agitated. As I was telling her my story, she had struggled mightily to avoid revealing her anxiety, too proud to show her true feelings. She had grown even paler and chewed on her lower lip. But the most astonishing thing was the rapid beat of her heart which was clearly audible some two or three steps away, as is the case with an aneurysm. I thought for sure she would burst into tears at any moment but she managed to hold them in.

"Where is the scaffolding?" she said.

"What scaffolding?"

"Where he died."

"If you'd like to see it, I can take you there on our way out. But listen, what is your name?"

"It doesn't matter."

"What doesn't matter?"

"Nothing. I have no name!" she said sharply and made a move toward the door again.

"Wait a moment," I called to her. "You are certainly a strange little girl! I wish you only the best. I've been worrying about you ever since I saw you crying on the stairs yesterday. Your grandfather died in my arms and when he mentioned the Sixth Line with his last breath, I felt as if he were entrusting me with your care. I had a dream about him. I even held onto your books for you. And yet you're still so timid with me, so afraid. You're obviously very poor, and probably an orphan, perhaps even living with strangers. That's true, isn't it?"

I pleaded with her as gently as I could, not knowing why I cared so deeply about her feelings. I was oddly attracted to her, not just out of pity, but something else. Maybe it was her connection to Smith or my own curious fascination with her state of mind, but she had touched my feelings in a way that was impossible to resist. My words seemed to touch her and she looked at me with a new, softer expression, her eyes meeting mine for a long time. Then she lowered her head again in thought.

"Elena," she whispered suddenly.

"Your name is Elena?"

"Yes."

"Will you come and visit me sometimes?"

"I can't," she stammered. "I don't know." She stopped to think it over. Just then the chimes of a neighborhood clock began to sound. Her agitation returned instantly and she asked in a frightened voice, "What time is it?"

"It should be half past ten," I replied.

She let out a cry of terror and turned to go, but I stopped her again. "I can't just let you run off like this. What are you afraid of? Are you late for something?"

"Yes, yes, you have to let me go! I ran off. She'll beat me!" Her voice trembled as she struggled to break free from my grasp.

"Listen to me and stop struggling. I'm going to Vasilyevsky Island right now, to the Thirteenth Line. I'm late too so I'm going to take a carriage. Come along with me and you'll get there much faster than on foot."

"But you can't go where I live!" she cried with a look of terror that disfigured her features, just from the sheer thought of my seeing where she lived.

"Look, I told you I was going to the Thirteenth Line, not to where you live. Come with me, it'll be faster."

We hurried down the stairs and I hailed the first cab that appeared, a wretched affair, but Elena was evidently in such a hurry that she climbed in beside me. I made the mistake of asking her who it was that she was frightened of and she became so panicked that she nearly fell out of the carriage. After that I kept my questions to myself. It was certainly a mystery.

The carriage seats were extremely awkward to sit in and with each bump Elena grabbed hold of my coat with her dirty, freckled left hand to steady herself. With her other hand she held tightly to her books as if they were priceless treasures. After one particularly large bump, Elena suddenly exposed one leg and I was greatly surprised to discover that she wore nothing but a pair of torn old boots, with no stockings at all. Although it may have been an inappropriate remark given her anxious state, I couldn't resist commenting.

"You have no stockings on! How could you go out in such cold, damp weather with no stockings?"

"I don't have any," she answered abruptly.

"But surely you live with someone who could have found a pair of stockings for you to go out in!"

"This is the way I like it."

"But you could get sick. You could die!"

"So I'll die then."

She clearly did not want to answer my questions.

"That is where *he* died," I said, pointing to the street curb where the old man had taken his last breath.

She studied the area for a moment and turned to me suddenly. "For God's sake, don't follow me! I promise I'll come back and visit you as soon as I can, but please don't follow me!"

"Well, I've already told you I wouldn't and I won't. But what are you so afraid of? It hurts me to see you so frightened."

"I'm not afraid of anyone," she responded indignantly.

"But you said a little while ago that she would beat you."

"So let her beat me," she said defiantly with an astonishing mix of both arrogance and fear. "I don't care!"

Finally we crossed the bridge and arrived on Vasilyevsky Island. Elena told the driver to let her out at the corner of the Sixth Line and she jumped out before the carriage had come to a stop. She looked around fearfully.

"Drive away! Drive away!" she hollered to the driver and then looked at me.

"Don't come after me!" she implored and quickly darted around the corner.

I told the driver to go ahead, but after the carriage had gone a short distance, I told him to stop, paid him, and jumped down onto the pavement. I quickly walked back to the Sixth Line and caught a glimpse of Elena hurrying along the other side of the street. She stopped and looked back several times to make sure she was not being followed, but I was able to duck into a doorway and remain out of sight.

I debated with myself whether or not I should follow her and decided that I must. Hiding behind gates and lampposts, I was able to avoid being seen as she continued along the other side of the street. I resolved not to follow her into any house, but felt that I must discover in which house she lived. I was feeling as depressed as I had been when the old man's dog, Azorka, had died at his feet at Mueller's.

CHAPTER NINETEEN

We walked a long distance until we reached Maly Prospect. Elena was practically running. Finally she stopped and went into a small grocery shop.

I stopped and waited. "Surely this little girl doesn't live in that shop," I thought. A moment later she came out again, but instead of her books, she was carrying a small ceramic mug.

After walking a short distance more, she entered the gate of a nondescript stone building, a small, two-storied house painted a dingy yellow. In one of the three windows on the lower floor there was a miniature red coffin which indicated that an undertaker had his shop there. The second-floor windows were very small and completely square-shaped, with dismal green frames and pink cotton curtains barely visible behind the dirty glass.

I crossed the street and approached the house in order to read a small sign which bore the words, "Madame Bubnova." I barely had time to register this information when a caustic female voice reverberated from inside the courtyard screaming curses at someone. I glanced in through the slats of the gate and saw a large, lower class peasant woman wearing a kerchief on her head and a green shawl. Her face was an appalling purplish color and her bloodshot eyes had a fierce look in them. In spite of the early hour it was clear that she was already intoxicated and she was scolding Elena, who cowered beneath her clutching the ceramic mug in front of her.

A thickly rouged and powdered woman stood watching from the stairs behind them and a moment later other faces began to appear. One, a pleasant but disheveled looking woman in a modest dress, appeared through a basement door, and from another door came an old man and a young girl. A tall, heavyset man carrying a broom stopped his work in the yard and turned his attention to the scene before him.

"Oh, you bloodsucking little shit," the purple woman screamed, releasing a stream of obscene curses that poured from her vile mouth without a single pause for breathe.

Finally, gagging for air, the woman turned to her neighbors and cried, "I sent her to the shop for cucumbers and she ran away! I yanked her hair out yesterday for pulling the same stunt and she does it again today. She rips out my heart when she disappears." She turned again to the tiny girl and continued. "Where do you go? Who are you seeing? Tell me, you venomous little snake, you monstrous mediocrity, or I'll kill you!"

The woman threw herself angrily on the girl and lashed out at her with her fists. When it looked as if one of her neighbors might intervene, the woman stopped and waved her hands frantically, as if giving testimony in her own defense. "You've seen it for yourselves," she screamed to the growing crowd. "This ungrateful little monster repays my saintly kindness with lies and deception. Me, who took her in off the streets when her mother died. None of you lifted a finger to help. You've barely enough to eat for yourselves. But I took her into my home and you see how she repays me. Sucking me dry like a blood-thirsty mosquito. For two months she's been like a rabid animal, vermin feeding on my flesh."

She turned again to the girl and screeched, "Leech! Parasite! You stubborn little bastard! Silence. That's all I get from you, even when I beat you. Not a single word. Silence! My heart breaks. Silence! Why do you treat me like this, with such contempt? Without me, you'd be living on the streets, dying of starvation. You should be bathing my feet with kisses, you thankless creature."

"Why are you so angry, Anna Trifonovna?" the rouged woman on the stairs asked cautiously. "What has she done to get you so worked up?"

"What has she done you ask? My dear friend, you know what a good woman I am. I don't bother other people with my troubles. But this ungrateful orphan will send me to an early grave. I sent her to the shop for cucumbers and she returned three hours later! Can you imagine how worried I was? My heart ached, it ached! Ached! Ached!" She turned again to the girl. "Where have you been? Who are you seeing? What new friend have you found? Am I not friend enough? Didn't I forgive your mother's debt of fourteen rubles and even pay to have her buried at my own expense?" She turned to the woman in the basement doorway. "My dear, you are a woman, you understand, you know! Doesn't such benevolence deserve some kindness in return? But she disobeys me. I've tried to make her happy. Didn't I clothe this scrawny scarecrow in a muslin dress and give her shoes fit for a holiday? And see what she's done, dear people. Within two days, the dress was torn to shreds and she ran off again. And didn't I catch her tearing the dress on purpose with her own two hands? 'I want to wear cotton,' she tells me, 'not muslin!' For that I made her scrub the floors, but she ran off again. I beat her something fierce when she returned and took away her stockings and shoes. 'She can't go out in bare feet,' I thought, but off she runs again and returns in these scruffy boots she stole from someone's trash. Where have you been sneaking off to, you evil spawn of Satan? Speak, you putrid pile of dung."

The harpy suddenly grabbed Elena's hair and drew her closer. The mug crashed to the ground, scattering the cucumbers across the yard, infuriating the woman even more. With a frenzied passion, the woman lashed out at the girl, beating her about the face and head, but Elena remained stubbornly silent, making no cry or complaint and making no effort to evade the woman's flailing fists.

I rushed through the gate and charged at the drunken woman. "What are you doing?" I screamed. "How dare you treat a defenseless child like that?" I grabbed for the woman's arm and pulled her off the girl.

"What's that?" the woman squawked, letting go of Elena and standing with her fists on her hips. "Who the hell are you? This is my house!"

"That doesn't give you the right to bully a poor orphan. She's not even yours. I heard you say that she was only staying with you!"

"Lord Jesus!" she screamed. "What the... did you come here with her? Are you the one she goes to see? You have no right to come to my house and attack me. I'll have the law on you! Help! Help me, I'm being attacked!"

Suddenly, she rushed at me with her fists flying. At that moment there was a shrill, inhuman wail and I turned to see Elena, who a moment before had been standing like a statue, fall to the ground and begin to writhe in a fit of epileptic convulsions. The disheveled looking woman, followed by another young girl, hurried to Elena, lifted her in her arms and carried her down the steps and into the building.

"Go ahead and shake, damn you," the crone shrieked as Elena disappeared into the house. "That's the third attack this month. She does it to irritate me!" The woman turned again and rushed at me. As I tried to hold her off, she called to the man with the broom. "Why are you standing there, you idler? I pay you good money! Help me!"

The lazy porter made a half-hearted attempt to earn his pay by calling out to me, "See here now, go away. Don't poke your nose around here!" He waved his broom in the air. "If you don't want a beating, just bow and take your leave."

There seemed to be nothing else for me to do, so I went to the gate and opened it. My outburst had been completely useless and yet fury still raged within me as I made my way to the sidewalk.

As I passed through the gate, I turned and looked back into the yard. The woman hurried up the stairs and into the house and the man with the broom, having earned his day's wages, disappeared around the corner of the building.

A moment later, the woman who had carried Elena into the basement apartment came up the steps. Seeing me, she stopped and looked at me curiously. Her kind and quiet demeanor encouraged me to venture back into the yard and address her directly. "May I ask you," I said, "who that little girl is and how she came to be living with that cruel woman? Please don't think I ask out of mere curiosity. I've met this child before and her living conditions are of great interest to me."

"Well, if you're interested in her well-being," the woman said quietly, as if afraid to be heard by others, "you'd better take her home with you and get her out of this place, that's for sure." She turned and started back down the steps.

"But if you won't answer my questions, how can I help her? I don't know anything about her. Am I right that that woman was Madame Bubnova herself, the mistress of the house?"

"Yes."

"But how did the little girl end up in her clutches. Did her mother die here?"

"I don't want to say anything. It's none of my business." She started to walk away again.

"Please," I called to her. "Help me. I'd like to do something for the girl but I need to know who she is. Who was her mother? Do you know?"

"She was a foreigner, I think. Spoke with an accent. She was living downstairs with us, but she was very sick and died of consumption."

"Then she must have been very poor, sharing a room in a basement..."

"Oh, yes, poor thing! Our hearts went out to her. We're struggling ourselves and she owed us six rubles for the five months she stayed with us. But we paid for her funeral and my husband made the coffin they buried her in."

"But that Bubnova woman said she paid for the funeral."

"Humph," the woman snorted with indignation.

"What was the mother's last name?" I asked.

"Oh, I can't pronounce it, sir. It was German, I think."

"Smith?"

"No, that's not it. Anna Trifonovna insisted on taking the child in to live with *her*, but it's just not right. Not right at all."

"But she must have had some reason to adopt the girl..."

"For no good reason, that's for sure," the woman said. She looked around nervously, afraid she might have been overheard. "We are outsiders, sir. It's none of our business."

"You'd better watch your tongue, woman," I heard a man behind her say. He was wearing a full coat over a dressing gown and looked like a craftsman, the woman's husband.

"She has no right speaking to you about something that's none of our business," the man said to me, glancing in the direction of Madame Bubnova's door. "We're coffin makers and if you ever have need of our services I'm sure we can satisfy your requirements. But until then, we have nothing to say. Good day, sir."

I turned and walked away from the house in deep thought, angry with myself for being unable to help the girl. Something the coffin-maker's wife had said made me very uneasy and fearful for the child's safety.

As I started down the sidewalk, I heard a man's voice call my name. I turned and saw a rowdy-looking drunk staggering towards me. Although he was dressed neatly, his coat was ragged and his cap was greasy. In spite of my initial revulsion, there was something about him that seemed familiar. He winked at me and grinned broadly.

"Don't you recognize me?"

CHAPTER TWENTY

"Yes, it's you, Masloboyev!" I cried, suddenly recognizing my old classmate from our provincial high school. "This is a surprise meeting."

"A surprise meeting indeed. Six years we haven't met. Although we've actually met several times, but your excellency did not deign to glance in my direction. After all, you are a general, sir. At least, a literary general, that is."

Saying this, he smiled ironically.

"Well, my friend, Masloboyev," I said, "that is not true. First of all, if there are literary generals, I am no more than a foot soldier, and second, let me tell you that I recall several times seeing you on the street, but you yourself seemed to be ignoring me. Why should I acknowledge a man who is trying to avoid me? And you know what I think? If you were not drunk right now, you probably wouldn't have called out to me as you did. I'm right, aren't I? Well, either way, hello! I'm very happy to see you again."

"Really? You mean you're not embarrassed to be seen in the company of a man dressed as I am? Well, you needn't answer that, it doesn't matter. You were always a very pleasant fellow, as I recall. You even got into a fight once defending me, but instead of thanking you I made fun of you for being such a fool. You were such an innocent soul! But hello, my dear friend, hello!"

He embraced me and kissed my cheek.

"All these years I've been thinking about you, dear Vanya, pining away, day and night, night and day. You're not an easy man to forget! But tell me, what have you been up to all this time?"

"Oh, well, I've been pining away too."

He gazed at me with a look of strong affection, clearly under the influence of too much wine, but he had always been a pleasant fellow even when sober.

"No, Vanya," he said in a surprisingly somber tone. "Your situation is nothing like mine!" A moment later, he brightened and announced, "By the way, Vanya, I read it. I read it. We should have a long talk. Are you in a hurry?"

"I am in a hurry, I must confess," I said, "and should tell you that I'm terribly upset about something. But I've got a better plan. Where do you live?"

"I'd be happy to tell you but that's certainly *not* a better plan. But can I tell you something that *would* be better?"

"Of course, what?"

"Look there, see?" He pointed to a sign about ten paces from where we were standing. "See? A confectioner's and restaurant. It's really just a simple café, but the atmosphere is warm and pleasant, decent food, and the vodka is unspeakably good! It's traveled all the way from Kiev on foot! I've sampled it many, many times and they wouldn't dare try to push anything inferior on me. They know Philip Philippich! I'm Philip Philippich! What? Why are you grinning? No, let me tell you what I propose. It's a quarter past eleven now—I've just checked—and at exactly 11:35, I'll let you go. Meanwhile, we'll raise a few glasses. Twenty minutes for an old friend, that's fair isn't it?"

"If it really is only twenty minutes, I'll join you, but I swear to you, I really am very busy."

"Ah, so we have a plan! But first, a few words. You do not look at all happy. Has something happened just recently to upset you?"

"Yes."

"That's what I thought. I have been learning Physiognomy, the science of reading facial characteristics and body language and I have been practicing on you! So, let's go, let's talk. In twenty minutes, I'll have time to throw back some birch wine, a cocktail with orange bitters, a parfait d'amour, and maybe something of my own invention. I drink, old man, I drink, on holidays and on Sunday mornings before Mass. You needn't join me, of course, but if you do drink, I believe you would display a special nobility of the soul. But come! A word or two and then we'll part for another ten years. For I am not a worthy companion for you, my friend!"

"Well then, let us go quickly. Twenty minutes of conversation and then I must run."

To reach the restaurant we had to climb a long wooden staircase leading to the second floor, but halfway up we came upon two inebriated men who staggered to one side to let us pass. One of them was a beardless young man with just the hint of a mustache that did little to disguise his intensely stupid face. He was dressed like a dandy, but in such comic fashion that it seemed he was wearing someone else's clothes. He wore expensive rings on his fingers and a fancy stickpin in his tie and his hair was combed in a ludicrous style that pointed straight up. He kept smiling and giggling.

His companion was easily fifty years of age, short, fat and balding, with a flabby, drunken, pock-marked face and a pair of spectacles on a miniscule nose which resembled a ruby red button. He also wore an expensive-looking stickpin and his expression was immoral and malevolent as he gazed at us through eyes that were little more than slits. Apparently, they both knew Masloboyev, but the fat man, upon seeing my companion, screwed up his face in a nasty grimace, while the younger man offered some kind of fawning, sickeningly sweet smile. He even took off his cap.

"Excuse me, Philip Philippich," he muttered, gazing fondly at Masloboyev.

"What?"

"Excuse me, sir," he said again as he flicked at his collar. "Mitroshka is sitting up there. It seems, Philip Philippich, sir, that he is a scoundrel."

"Why do you say that?"

"It's because, sir, last week Mitroshka smeared my friend's face with sour cream in a very indecent way." He suddenly hiccupped loudly.

The other man angrily poked him with his elbow.

"Come join us, Philip Philippich, and we'll down another half-dozen drinks in your honor. What do you say?"

"No, sir, that I cannot do," Masloboyev replied. "I have business."

The young man hiccupped again. "And I have business which concerns you." His fat friend once again nudged him with his elbow and he responded angrily. "Later! Later!"

Masloboyev did his best to avoid looking at the two men as we eased past them on the staircase. We entered the first room and discovered a long counter heavily laden with cakes, pies, pastries and succulent treats of every variety accompanied by glass decanters of multi-colored liqueurs. Masloboyev grabbed me and quickly pulled me into a corner.

"That young man is the son of Sizobryukhov who made a fortune raising meadowsweet. The boy inherited half-a-million rubles when his father died and he's been carousing ever since. He returned after months in Paris with almost nothing left in his pocket and then turned around and inherited another fortune from his uncle. So here he is, trying to squander the rest. A year from now, he'll be passing the hat around. He's as stupid as a goose but is seen in the finest restaurants, cellars and taverns with actresses on his arm, and he recently applied for a commission in the mounted cavalry. The older man is Arkhipov, a merchant or manager or, perhaps, a government procurer, but he is most certainly a rogue and a rascal and presently Sizobryukhov's closest friend. He is Falstaff and Judas combined, twice bankrupt, and a degenerate, licentious creature with perverse tastes. I know of at least one criminal incident in which he was implicated, but he bought his way out of it. I'm actually very glad that we have run into Arkhipov as I've got a bone to pick with him. He is, of course, robbing Sizobryukhov blind. He knows every little corner in the city where foolish young men like to congregate. That's why he's so useful to the boy. Mitroshka is that dashing young man with the Gypsy face and the expensive velvet tunic standing over there by the window. He buys and sells horses but he is also a master con artist who could forge a note right before your eyes and still pass it on to you in a legitimate transaction. He's a true Slavophile, and I have to admit he pulls it off admirably, but dress him up in a proper dress coat and you could take him to the finest English club and pass him off as Count Barabanov. No one would see through the ruse. But he's likely to end up badly. His kind usually do. But as I was saying, Mitroshka dislikes the fat man even more than I do. Mitroshka and Sizobryukhov were very close until Arkhipov seduced the boy away before Mitroshka could fleece him. If the three of them met here in the restaurant, there must be something up. I even know what it is because Mitroshka himself told me that Arkhipov and Sizobryukhov would be hanging around here today. I came to take advantage of Mitroshka's hatred for Arkhipov because I have my own good reasons to feel the same way. I don't want Mitroshka to suspect, and don't keep staring at him, but when we leave here I expect Mitroshka to come running after us to tell me what I want to know. And now let us go, Vanya, into the other room."

As we walked, Masloboyev turned to a waiter and said, "Well now, Stephan, you understand what I need you to do?"

"Yes, sir, I do."

"And you'll take care of it?"

"Yes, sir."

"Wonderful. Come, Vanya, let's sit down. Why are you looking at me like that? I see you staring at me. Are you surprised? Don't be. Anything can happen to a man that he's never even dreamed of, even in the days when... Well, yes, when we crammed Latin together in school. Look, Vanya, believe in one thing. Masloboyev may have indeed strayed from the path, but his heart remains the same, only the circumstances have changed. Though I may be covered in soot, I'm no dirtier than the next man. I had planned to be a doctor and later a professor of Russian literature. I even wrote an article about Gogol. I was set to marry—every soul seeks sustenance in another— and she agreed, even though I was so poor I couldn't tempt a cat to live with me. I was preparing for the wedding ceremony and even borrowed a pair of boots to substitute for my own which had been in tatters for more than a year, but we never went through with the wedding. She married a teacher and I took a job as a clerk. Not even in a business office. It was... well, just an office. But then the music changed for me and I began to thrive. I may not be in government service but I have found it easy to amass money. I take a bribe now and then, but I am an honest man. I feed with the sheep but run with the wolves. And I have learned the rules. For example, there is safety in numbers but keep your secrets to yourself. I deal in matters of confidentiality. Do you understand?"

"I think so. Are you some kind of detective?"

"No, not really a detective, but I do take on some cases, more as an avocation than vocation. And yet I am a professional. You see, Vanya, I drink vodka. Never so much that I lose my senses and throw away my future. But *my* day is past. You can't decorate an egg once it's broken. One thing I will say is this, if there were not still a little of the old me rattling around inside I should never have approached you on the street. It's true, I have seen you before, many times, and have wanted to say hello but I didn't dare. I kept putting it off because I am not worthy of you. You were right before, Vanya, when you said I wouldn't have spoken to you if I weren't drunk. But I'm just prattling on about nonsense. I'd much rather talk about you.

Well, my dear soul, I've read it. Read it! I am referring, of course, to your first born. As I read it, I almost felt myself becoming a better person! Almost, yes, but I thought better of it and preferred to stay a dishonorable man. So there you have it."

As he prattled on, he grew progressively drunker and began to weep at his own maudlin tales. Masloboyev had always been a nice enough fellow in school but he had a sly and cunning mind that developed early. He had a good heart but he was a lost man. There are a great many other Russian people like him. They are more than capable, but live their lives in a chaotic, confused state, consciously fighting against their conscience, either out of weakness or misguided determination, and always ending up in wreckage, even though they knew beforehand they were heading down the path to ruin. Masloboyev, for example, had chosen to drown himself in vodka.

"Now, my friend," Masloboyev continued, "only one word more. I heard the thunder that greeted your new found fame and then I read your critics. Yes, I know you imagine that I read nothing. Then I saw you in the street wearing a battered hat and shabby boots, traipsing through the mud without galoshes, and I drew my own conclusions. You've taken up journalism as a trade now, am I right?"

"Yes, Masloboyev."

"So, you've joined the literary hacks."

"Looks like it."

"Well, my boy, here's what I say: drink is better! Here I can lie down on a sofa—and I have a nice couch with springs—and imagine myself to be Homer or Dante or a Roman Emperor. One can imagine whatever one wishes. But you cannot imagine yourself Homer or Dante or a Roman Emperor, firstly because you want to be yourself and secondly because all you desire is forbidden to you as a literary hack. I have a good imagination and you have only reality. Tell me openly and honestly as a brother—and if you won't speak as a brother, you will offend and humiliate me for ten years—you like money, don't you? I have more than enough. Stop making faces at me. Take a little money and pay off the debtors. Get rid of the burden and when you put aside enough to last a year, sit down with your favorite idea and write a great book! Eh? What do you think?"

"Listen, Masloboyev! I appreciate your brotherly offer, but I can't give you my answer right now. The reason why is a long story. There are circumstances. However, I promise I will tell you later and we will speak like brothers. Thank you for the advice. I promise that I will come to you and come many times. But here's the thing. You are frank with me and therefore I dare ask your advice on a matter about which you are quite knowledgeable."

And I told him the whole story of Smith and his granddaughter, starting with the scene in Mueller's pastry shop. Oddly enough, as I told him my story a look in his eyes told me that he already knew something. I asked him about it.

"No, no, it's nothing really," he answered. "Although I had heard *something* about Smith, about an old man dying outside a pastry shop. It's really this Madame Bubnova that I know something about. Just two months ago I managed to get some money out of her. *Je prends mon bien partout où je le trouve*, which is probably the only thing I have in common with Molière. But even though I squeezed a hundred rubles out of her, I promised myself I wouldn't settle for less than another five hundred. Nasty woman! She runs a most unsavory kind of business. Normally that wouldn't matter to me, but she takes it to extremes. Don't imagine me a Don Quixote. The point is that I can take advantage of circumstances and when, half an hour ago, I ran into Sizobryukhov, I was very pleased. Sizobryukhov apparently was brought here, and brought here by the fat man, and as I know the kind of profession the fat man trades in, I drew my own conclusions. Well, yes, I really have this covered! I am very glad you told me about this young girl, it puts me on the right track. I am engaged in a variety of private commissions for some very peculiar people. I was recently looking into a matter for a prince, and let me tell you that this is not the sort of thing one would expect from a prince. And then, do you want to hear another story about a married woman? You come visit me some time, brother, and I'll tell you some stories that you would not believe."

"And what was the name of this prince?" I interrupted him, with an uncomfortable premonition.

"Why do you need to know? Oh, very well. His name is Valkovsky."

"Peter?"

"Yes. Do you know him?"

"Yes, but not very well," I said, getting to my feet. "Well, Masloboyev, I shall ask you more about this gentleman very soon. You have definitely aroused my interest."

"Well, old friend, you may visit me as often as you want. I have many interesting stories to tell, but within certain limits, you understand? I can't afford to be indiscreet and lose my honor. It's not good for business."

"Of course. Only as far as your *honor* will allow."

I was very excited and he noticed it.

"But what about the story I've just told you. Has it made you think of something?"

"About your story?"

"Yes. But wait two minutes for me. I will pay."

He walked over to the buffet and, as if by accident, suddenly found himself standing near the man in the velvet tunic whom he had so unceremoniously called Mitroshka. It seemed to me that Masloboyev knew him a little more intimately than he had admitted to me. It was evident, at least, that they were not meeting for the first time.

Mitroshka was an uncommonly distinct-looking young man. In his tunic and red silk shirt, with sharp well-formed features and a still youthful, dark-skinned complexion and bold flashing eyes, he made a curious but not unappealing impression. His gestures suggested a restless, nervous personality, but at that moment he seemed to be restraining himself, perhaps anxious to project an image of extreme efficiency and reliability.

"Look, Vanya," Masloboyev said when he returned to me. "Come see me at seven o'clock this evening and I may have something to tell you. On my own, as you can see, I have nothing to offer you. In the old days, maybe, but now I am nothing but a drunk. But I still have connections who can be most useful. A little piece of information from one, a bit more from another, and that is how I survive. In my free time, you see, I investigate certain matters. But that's enough for now. Here's my address on Shestilavochnaya Street. Right now, brother, I am too drunk. I'll have one more and then head on home. You come by this evening and I'll introduce you to Alexandra Semyonovna and we can talk about poetry."

"But what about that other matter?"

"Well, yes, that too, perhaps."

"Then, perhaps, I will come. Yes, I will come."

CHAPTER TWENTY-ONE

Anna Andreyevna had been expecting me for a long time. Ever since I had told her about Natasha's note the day before, she was eager to learn more. She had been waiting for me since ten o'clock that morning, so by the time I arrived at two o'clock the poor woman's anxiety had reached a fever pitch. In addition, she wanted to tell me about her budding hopes since yesterday and that Nikolai Sergeich was sick and feeling gloomy, and yet he was also being particularly gentle with her. When I arrived she was clearly unhappy with me. Her teeth were clenched and her cold and indifferent expression seemed to be saying, "Why do you come here every day?" She was clearly angry at my late arrival. But I was in a hurry and without further delay I described yesterday's scene with Natasha. As soon as the old woman heard about the older prince's visit and his solemn proposal, she immediately dropped her feigned displeasure. I can't find words to describe how happy she was, barely able to contain herself. She wept and crossed herself, bowed to me on her knees, hugged me, and wanted to rush to Nikolai Sergeich and tell him of her joy.

"Have mercy, sir, he has been made ill from the humiliation and insults he has endured, but when he finds out that Natasha has been exonerated, he will forget it all at once."

I had a difficult time dissuading her. The dear old woman had lived with her husband for twenty-five years and yet knew so little about him. She was anxious, as well, to go with me immediately to Natasha. I convinced her that not only might Nikolai Sergeich disapprove of her actions, she might also damage the situation by going. With difficulty, she changed her mind, but kept me half an hour extra and kept on talking the whole time.

"How can I just sit here alone in four walls with such joy in my heart?"

Finally, I persuaded her to let me go alone, reminding her that Natasha had been waiting impatiently for me. The old woman crossed herself several more times to bless my journey and sent a special blessing with me to Natasha. I told her I would absolutely not return again that evening unless there was something new to report about Natasha. I didn't see Nicolai Sergeich at all on that visit. He had not slept the previous night, complaining of a headache and chills, and was now asleep in his study.

Natasha had also been waiting for me all morning. When I entered the room she was, as usual, pacing up and down, anxiously rubbing her hands together as though in meditation. Even now, when I think back on it, I can see her in that poor room, dreamy, deserted, waiting with folded hands and downcast eyes, walking aimlessly back and forth.

As she continued to pace she asked me quietly why I was so late? I told her briefly of my many adventures, but she didn't seem to be listening. It was clear that she was very concerned about something.

"Anything new?" I asked.

"Nothing new," she replied, but I could see immediately from her expression that she had new information she was eager to reveal but, as usual, she would not tell me until I was just about to leave. That's the way she was and I was used to it.

We began, of course, to talk about yesterday. I was particularly struck by the fact that we agreed completely with each other in our impression of Prince Valkovsky. She positively disliked him, even more than she had yesterday. As we discussed his visit, Natasha suddenly said, "Listen, Vanya, it always happens that when people meet someone they don't like at first, that it's really a sign that they *will* like them later. At least, that's the way it usually works with me."

"God willing, Natasha. And that's my opinion, and it's the final one. I've been thinking about the prince and he seems devoutly religious, so perhaps he was quite serious when he agreed to your marriage."

Natasha stopped in the middle of the room and looked at me sternly. Her face changed, her lips quivered slightly.

"But in a case like this," she said with astonishment, "how could he have been deceiving... lying?"

"Yes, of course, that's right!" I agreed quickly.

"Of course he wasn't lying. There is nothing to even think about. There could be no excuse for such deception. How could he look me in the eyes as he did and be mocking me? Could any man be capable of such an insult?"

"No, of course not," I confirmed, and thought to myself: "You poor girl, you can't think of anything else as you pace back and forth and, perhaps, you're even more in doubt than I am."

"Oh, how I wish he would return soon!" she said. "He wanted to spend the whole evening with me, and then... He must have important business to do or he wouldn't have gone away. Do you know what it is, Vanya? Have you heard anything?"

"God only knows. After all, the prince is always making money. I've heard he's taken a share in some contract in St. Petersburg. The affairs of business mean nothing to us, Natasha."

"Of course, nothing at all. Alyosha mentioned some letter yesterday."

"News of some sort. Has Alexey been here?"

"Yes."

"Early?"

"At noon. He likes to sleep late. He sat for a while and then I chased him to Katerina Fedorovna. That was the right thing to do, wasn't it, Vanya?"

"Why, wasn't he planning to go there anyway?"

"Yes, he was going..."

She wanted to say something else but stopped. I looked at her and waited. Her face was sad. I would have asked her, but she sometimes disliked being questioned.

"He's a strange boy," she said finally, her mouth twisted slightly as if trying not to look at me.

"Why do you say that? Have you heard something?"

"No, nothing, but... He was very sweet, I thought. Only I..."

"Now all of his troubles and worries are over," I said.

Natasha looked intently and searchingly at me. She may have been tempted to reply, "He had very few sorrows and cares before," but it seemed to her that my words conveyed the same idea. She pouted.

A moment later, however, she was gracious and polite again. This time she was exceptionally gentle. I stayed with her for over an hour. She was very worried. Valkovsky had frightened her. I noticed from some of her questions that she wanted to know if she had made a favorable impression on him yesterday. How had she behaved? Had she expressed too much joy? Was she too ill-tempered? Or, conversely, too appeasing? She didn't want him to misjudge her. Or to laugh at her. Or to feel contempt for her. Her cheeks flushed like fire at the thought.

"How can you get so upset by what you imagine some evil man might think of you? Let him think what he wants," I said.

"Why is he evil?" she asked.

Natasha was apprehensive, but her heart was pure and honest. Any mistrust on her part came from a clear conscience. She was proud and noble, and her pride could not endure having someone she thought superior made to look ridiculous in her own eyes. Contempt from an inferior, of course, would have been met with her own contempt, but her heart ached at the thought of mockery of something or someone she considered holy, no matter who was doing the laughing. It wasn't from a lack of firmness on her part. It arose from too little knowledge of the world and being unaccustomed to other people, having been closed up in her own little world. She had spent her life in the safety of her own corner. And finally, that trait present in most good-natured people, perhaps inherited from her father, of stubbornly believing that people are better than they are, exaggerating their positive qualities, was strongly developed in her. It is difficult for such individuals to deal with later disappointments, even more so when they feel somehow guilty. Why expect more from people than they can give? But disappointment is always awaiting these people. It is best to sit quietly in their corners and not venture into the light. I have even noticed that they come to love their corners and grow increasingly unsociable. Natasha, however, had suffered many misfortunes, many insults. She was a wounded creature and could not be blamed, if any of my words sounded accusatory.

But I was in a hurry and got up to go. She gasped and almost started crying at the thought of my leaving, even though all the time I had been sitting there she had shown me no special tenderness; quite the contrary, in fact, she had seemed colder than usual. She kissed me passionately and then looked into my eyes for a long time.

"Listen," she said. "Alyosha was quite bizarre today and even surprised me. He was very nice, very happy, but he flew in like a butterfly, so self-possessed, spinning around and admiring himself in the mirror. He's a little too brusque now... Yes, and he stayed only a short time. Imagine. He brought me candy."

"Candy? Well, that's very sweet and simple-minded. Oh, the two of you! You've started watching and spying on each other, trying to read each other's secret thoughts, and understanding nothing. He hasn't changed. He's just as cheerful and schoolboyish as ever. But you... there's something different about you... something!"

As always, when Natasha changed her tone and approached me to complain about Alyosha or to confer about an embarrassing misunderstanding or reveal some secret, always expecting me to understand her with half a word, she would look at me with a grin, as if begging me to say something that would immediately set her heart at rest. But I remember, too, in those instances, how I always took on a stern and harsh tone, as if scolding her, and (although I did it quite unintentionally), it always worked. The severity and importance of my words were effective; they seemed more authoritative, and sometimes a person just feels an irresistible need to be scolded. Natasha was often quite comforted.

"No, Vanya," she said, staring into my eyes with one of her little hands on my shoulder and the other clutching my own hand. "I thought he seemed somehow more... you know, affected. As though we'd been married ten years, but he was still being polite to his wife. Am I reading too much into this? He laughed and spun around, but somehow it seemed to be only partly about me, not like it was before. He was in a hurry to see Katerina Fedorovna. I spoke to him but he wasn't listening and started talking about something else; you know, that grand, nasty habit aristocrats have that we've both worked so hard to wean out of him. In short, he was... he seemed indifferent... But look what I'm doing! Starting in again! Ah, we are so demanding, Vanya, such capricious despots! Only now I see it! I can't accept even the slightest change in his face when only God knows why his face has changed! You were right, Vanya, to reproach me just now! This is all my fault! I create my own bitterness and then complain about it. Thank you, Vanya, you have comforted me completely. Ah, if only he would come again today! But maybe he would be angry about what happened this morning."

"But you didn't really quarrel, did you?" I asked in amazement.

"No, I revealed nothing! But I was a little sad, and although he acted so cheerful and thoughtful, I thought his good-bye was a bit cold. Yes, I will send for him. And you will come, too, Vanya. Today!"

"Certainly, unless something delays me."

"Why, what something is that?"

"Oh, it's just something I've imposed on myself! At any rate, it seems that I must come!"

CHAPTER TWENTY-TWO

At seven o'clock I was at Masloboyev's. He lived in a small house on Shestilavochnaya Street in a rather untidy, though not poorly furnished, apartment made up of three rooms. There were some signs of prosperity but an overall look of disarray. The door was opened by a very pretty girl of nineteen, very simple, but very nicely dressed, neat and with friendly, welcoming eyes. I immediately realized that this was Alexandra Semyonovna, the young wife he had mentioned in passing that morning, hinting that I would be delighted to meet her. She asked who I was and upon hearing my name told me Masloboyev was waiting for me, but that he was sleeping in his room. She led me there and I found Masloboyev asleep on a beautiful, soft sofa, covered with his dirty overcoat, his head on a leather bag. Just as we entered, he awoke from a light sleep and called me by name.

"Ah, Vanya, is that you? I've been waiting for you. Just now in my dream you came and woke me. So, it's time. Let's go."

"Go? Where to?"

"To see a lady."

"What lady? Why?"

"To Madame Bubnova, to break up her little party. Ah, such a beauty," he said, turning to Alexandra Semyonovna and kissing his fingertips at the thought of Madame Bubnova.

"Oh, you're making that up!" the girl said, as if it was her duty to pretend to be angry.

"Have you two met? Alexandra Semyonovna, I'm honored to present Ivan Petrovich, a literary general. It is only once a year you can inspect him for nothing. Any other time you would have to pay."

"There, he's playing the fool again," she said to me. "Please don't listen to him. He's always making fun of me. What kind of a general could this man be?"

"I'm trying to tell you," Masloboyev said, "He's a very special kind. And you, your Excellency, do not imagine that we are foolish. We are much smarter than we seem at first glance."

"Don't listen to him! He's always trying to embarrass me in front of other people. He's shameless. If only he would take me to the theater once in a while!"

"No, Alexandra Semyonovna, love your home. Do not forget that you must love... something. Have you forgotten the word I taught you?"

"Of course I haven't forgotten. It means... some nonsense."

"Well, what was the word then?"

"I'm not going to embarrass myself in front of a guest. It's probably something naughty. I'm not going to say it."

"So you *have* forgotten the word."

"No, I haven't! Penates... love your Penates. Why should I love them? It's all lies!"

"Yes, Penates. Love your hearth and home. But at Madame Bubnova's..."

"Damn you and your Bubnova!" she said and ran from the room with great indignation.

"It's time to go! Farewell, Alexandra Semyonovna," he called to her as we left.

"See here, Vanya, first let's grab this cab. There now. And secondly, I learned something after I said good-bye earlier; it's no longer just a hunch, but a certainty. I stayed on Vasilyevsky Island for another hour. That fat man is a terrible scoundrel, filthy, ugly, and with vile and perverse tastes. I've known for a long time that he and Bubnova were in business together. She recently got hold of a girl from a respectable family. That muslin dress you mentioned this morning when you spoke about the orphan made me very uneasy because I had already heard something about it before. I've just now learned something else, quite by accident, but it seems likely. How old is this girl?"

"From how she looks, I'd say thirteen."

"But small for her age. That sounds about right. If necessary, she'll say she's eleven; another time, fifteen. And since the poor thing has no protection, no family, then..."

"Do you mean...?"

"What do you think? Yes. Madame Bubnova would never have taken in an orphan out of compassion. And if the fat man is involved in this, it's definitely true. He visited Bubnova this morning. He promised that blockhead Sizobryukhov a beautiful married woman today, the wife of an official at headquarters. These rich boys are always inclined to prefer a higher class. It's like in Latin grammar, remember, where prominence takes precedence?" Masloboyev paused a moment. "I think I'm still drunk from this morning. Bubnova doesn't usually involve herself in such nasty business, but she thinks she can fool the police by claiming she's adopted the girl, but I'm on to her! I can throw a scare into her because she remembers me well... And that's the story. Do you understand?"

I was quite shaken up by these revelations and feared that we would be too late, so I urged the cabman to hurry.

"Don't worry, Vanya," Masloboyev assured me, "measures have been taken. Mitroshka is there already. Sizobryukhov will pay with cash, but that pot-bellied scoundrel will pay with his skin. That was decided this morning. And I'll take care of Bubnova... Because she doesn't dare to..."

We arrived at the restaurant and stopped, but the man called Mitroshka was not there. We ordered the coachman to wait at the restaurant and hurried to Madame Bubnova's on foot. Mitroshka was waiting for us at the gate. Bright light streamed from the windows of the house and we could hear the sound of Sizobryukhov's drunken laughter.

"They've been up there for a quarter of an hour," Mitroshka told us. "It's time."

"But how can we get in?" I asked.

"As guests," Masloboyev said. "She knows me and she knows Mitroshka, as well. The doors may be locked, but not to us."

He knocked quietly on the gate and it was opened immediately by the porter, who exchanged winks with Mitroshka. We walked quietly so we would not be heard inside. The porter took us up the steps and knocked. His name was called from within and he answered, "There is someone here to see you!"

The door opened and we all went in at once. The porter disappeared.

"Yes?" Madame Bubnova whined. "Who is it?" She was drunk and unkempt and stood before us with a tiny candle in her hands.

"Who is it? How can you ask such a thing, Anna Trifonovna? Don't you recognize your honored guest? Who, if not me? Philip Philippich!"

"Ah, Philip Philippich! It is you. But who are your... Why are you...? Please come in, sir."

She was quite flustered.

"Where?" Masloboyev asked. "In here? But there is a partition... No, we would prefer the next room. Are there no lovelies to welcome us?"

The hostess instantly collected herself.

"Yes, for such honored guests, I would dig all the way to China for them."

"Three words, my dear Anna Trifonovna. Is Sizobryukhov here?"

"Yes. In there."

"Ah, just the man I'm looking for. How dare that scalawag run off on a drunken spree without inviting me?"

"I don't think he's forgotten. He's been expecting someone. It must be you."

Masloboyev pushed open the door and we found ourselves in a small room with two windows decorated with geraniums, several wicker chairs and a battered old upright piano; just the sort of atmosphere one would expect from such an establishment. But even before we entered, even while we were still talking in the hall, Mitroshka had vanished. I learned later why he had not joined us, but had been met at another door by the thickly rouged woman I had seen behind Bubnova that morning. They were, apparently, very good friends.

Sizobryukhov was sitting on a slender mahogany sofa in front of a round table covered with a cloth. On the table were two bottles of warm champagne and a cheap bottle of rum. There were plates of baked sweets, cakes and nuts of three varieties. Sitting at the table, opposite Sizobryukhov, was a disgusting, pockmarked creature of some forty years in a black taffeta dress with bronze bracelets and brooches. She was, all too obviously, the fake "officer's wife," but Sizobryukhov was drunk and seemed perfectly content. His fat companion was not with him.

"So this is the way I find you!" Masloboyev roared with laughter. "And after you invited us to Dussot's!"

"Philip Philippich, what a pleasure!" Sizobryukhov muttered, standing to greet us with a blissful expression.

"Have you been drinking?" Masloboyev asked.

"Excuse me, sir."

"No need to apologize, but you could invite your guests to join you. We may have to catch up. I've brought another guest, a friend!"

Masloboyev pointed to me.

"Pleased, sir, to make your... it's my pleasure to... Hic! Hey, you call this champagne? It tastes like sour cabbage soup."

"You offend me," said the officer's wife.

"So, you didn't dare show your face at Dussot's," Masloboyev bellowed. "And after inviting me!"

"He's been telling me that he's been to Paris," the woman said. "But I think he's lying!"

"Theodosia Titishna," Sizobryukhov whimpered. "You wound me. I was there. We went."

"But what would a peasant like him be doing in Paris?"

"We have! We could! I was there with Karp Vasilich. Do you know Karp Vasilich?"

"And why would I want to know Karp Vasilich?"

"Well, it's just... it could be beneficial to you. We were there in Paris, at Madame Joubert's. He broke a glass."

"He broke what?"

"A glass mirror. It stretched almost from floor to ceiling. Karp Vasilich was so drunk and he was prattling on in Russian with Madame Joubert and he leans his elbow against this big mirror. Madame Joubert shouted at him in her own language, 'Be careful! That glass cost me seven hundred francs!' That's four hundred rubles. 'You'll break it!' He just looked at me and grinned. I was sitting on a sofa across from him with a real beauty next to me; not a mutt like you, but a real knockout, that's the only word for her. And he called to me, 'Stephan Terentyevich. Shall we go halves?' And I said, 'Done!' So he took his fist and smashes it against the mirror. Bang! Splinters of glass flew everywhere. Joubert screamed and confronted him face to face. 'What are you, a hooligan?' In her own language, of course. And he told her: 'You, Madame, may have the money. I am no criminal.' And he immediately handed over six hundred and fifty francs. He disputed the other fifty."

At that moment, a terrible, piercing scream rang out two or three rooms from where we were. I shuddered and cried out as well because I recognized Elena's voice. Immediately after her plaintive cry, we heard more screams, curses, scuffling, and finally the clear, crisp sound of a palm slapping a face. It was probably Mitroshka resolving the situation in his own way. Suddenly the door flew open and Elena ran in, her face pale and eyes dim, wearing a torn and crumpled muslin dress. Her hair had been carefully brushed, but it now appeared tousled as if from a fight. I stood just inside the door and she ran straight to me and threw her arms around me. Everyone jumped up with alarm. There were more screams and cries from the other room. Suddenly, Mitroshka appeared in the doorway dragging by the hair his fat nemesis, who was now utterly disheveled. Mitroshka pushed Archipov across the threshold and flung him into the room.

"Here he is! Take him!" Mitroshka said with a look of complete satisfaction.

"Look," Masloboyev said, quietly coming up to me and tapping me on the shoulder. "Take our cab and take the girl to your home. There is nothing else for you to do here. We will settle the rest tomorrow."

I did not need to be told twice. I grabbed Elena's hand and took her out of that den. I still don't know how things ended there. No one tried to stop us. Madame Bubnova was struck with horror. It all happened so quickly that she didn't know what to do. The cab was still waiting and in twenty minutes we were at my apartment.

Elena was half-dead. I undid the hooks on her dress, sprinkled her face with water, and laid her on my bed. She had become feverish and was delirious. I looked at her pale face, her colorless lips, her dark, tangled hair which had earlier been brushed and pomaded but was now hanging down on one side, her entire getup with pink ribbons still attached here and there to her dress, and finally understood the whole ugly truth. Poor little thing! She was getting worse and worse. I did not want to leave her and decided not to go to Natasha's that evening. Occasionally, Elena opened her long, dark eyelashes and looked long and hard at me, as if she recognized me. It was past midnight when she finally dozed off. I fell asleep beside her on the floor.

CHAPTER TWENTY-THREE

I arose very early. During the night I kept waking up almost every half-hour. Each time I did, I went to my poor guest and watched carefully over her. She still had a fever and was slightly delirious. But toward morning, she fell into a sound sleep. A good sign, I thought, but decided to run for a doctor while she was still sleeping. I knew a doctor, a good-natured old man who from time immemorial had lived alone with his German housekeeper near Vladimir Square. I arrived at his door around eight and he promised to be at my room by ten o'clock. I wanted to stop to see Masloboyev on my way home but I thought better of it. I knew that Elena could wake up at any time and be frightened by her unfamiliar surroundings. In her depressed state of mind, she might not even remember how and when she had arrived at my apartment.

She opened her eyes at the very moment I entered the room. I approached her and gently asked how she felt. She did not answer, but for a long time stared at me with her large, expressive black eyes. It seemed to me from her gaze that she understood and was fully conscious but, as was her usual habit, she didn't answer me. Since her very first visit to my room she had displayed an obstinate pride whenever I questioned her, and she would stare at me with a mixture of both scorn and curiosity. I tried to put my hand on her forehead to see if she had a fever, but she silently and firmly removed my hand and turned her face to the wall. I moved away so I wouldn't disturb her.

I had a big copper kettle that I used instead of a samovar to boil water and, as usual, the building's porter had furnished me with enough wood to last for five days. I lit the stove, went to fetch some water and filled the kettle. As I prepared the table for tea service, Elena turned her head and watched me with curiosity. I asked her if she wanted anything but she immediately turned her face away again and said nothing.

"Why is she so angry?" I wondered. "Such a strange girl!"

As promised, my old doctor friend arrived at ten o'clock. He examined the patient with a German's attention for detail and reassured me that, although she still had a fever, Elena was in no particular danger. He did point out, however, that she seemed to have a chronic condition, something about an irregular heartbeat, that would require special observation. He wrote out a prescription for some medicine, more out of custom than necessity, and then immediately started asking me who she was and how she had come to be in my apartment. The old man was a chronic snoop.

Elena had had a striking effect on him. She had pulled her hand away from his when he attempted to take her pulse and refused to show him her tongue. She answered none of his questions, but gazed fixedly the entire time at the large Order of Saint Stanislaus pendant swinging from his neck. "Her head probably aches," the old man said, "and, my heaven, how she stares!"

I didn't think it was necessary to tell him much about Elena and assured him that it was a very long story.

"Let me know if you need me again," he said as he left. "At any rate, she is in no danger."

I decided to stay with Elena the whole day and remain close by her side as much as possible until she recovered. But knowing that Natasha and Anna Andreyevna would be upset if they waited all day in vain for me to show up, I decided to send a letter to Natasha telling her that I could not come that day. I could not write directly to her mother because Anna Andreyevna had told me not to send her any more letters after I had once sent her the news of Natasha's illness.

"The old man frowns when he sees a letter from you," she had told me. "He really wants to know what is in it but is too stubborn to ask, so he ends up cranky and upset the whole day. And besides, Vanya, a letter from you is such a tease. What can I learn from ten lines? I want to ask more but you're not here to ask!"

So I wrote only the one letter to Natasha and posted it on my way to the apothecary.

Meanwhile, Elena fell asleep again. In a dream, she moaned and shuddered slightly. The doctor had guessed correctly. She had a very bad headache. Occasionally, she cried out and woke up briefly. She glanced at me with great annoyance, as if it were especially difficult for her to be in my presence. I must confess, this was very painful to me.

Masloboyev came at eleven o'clock. He was preoccupied and seemed absent-minded and left in a hurry after only a minute.

"Well, my brother, I didn't expect to find you living in luxury," he said, looking around, "but this place is really little more than a trunk. It's a packing case, not an apartment. How can you write with all these outside distractions? I thought about it yesterday when we went to Bubnova's. I belong to a class of people who rarely do anything worthwhile, but you are different. Listen, I may come to visit you tomorrow or the next day, but you must certainly visit me on Sunday morning. By that time we may have a solution to this girl's case. I told you yesterday—well only hinted at it—but we will talk seriously, because you need to take this seriously. And finally, would it be too great a dishonor for you to accept a little money from me as a loan?"

"Don't worry about me," I interrupted him. "Just tell me what happened at Bubnova's last night after we left."

"Oh, that. Yes, that ended quite well, our goal was achieved. But I have no time now. I just came to see how you want to handle the situation with the girl."

"I don't know. I must confess I've been waiting to talk it over with you!"

"Oh. Well, have you considered keeping her here, as a servant?"

"Please keep your voice down," I said to him. "She's very ill but she *does* know what's going on around her. She looked startled when you arrived because I think it reminded her of what happened yesterday."

I proceeded to tell him what I knew about Elena's background and how I perceived her character. Masloboyev seemed very interested. I also told him I was hoping to find a house where Elena could live and mentioned the Ichmenyev family. To my great surprise, he was already partially acquainted with Natasha's history and I questioned how he knew.

"I've been hearing passing comments about her situation for some time," Masloboyev said. "I've already mentioned to you that I know about Prince Valkovsky. That's a good idea about setting her up with the old couple. She'll only cause you trouble here. Oh, and one more thing. She'll need proper papers, but don't worry about that, I'll take care of it. Farewell, come see me more often. Is she sleeping now?"

"I think so," I answered.

But as soon as he left, Elena immediately called to me.

"Who was that?" she asked. Her voice trembled, but she looked at me with that same intent and haughty expression. Other than that, she said nothing.

I told her Masloboyev's name and added that he had been responsible for helping me get her away from Madame Bubnova and that Bubnova was afraid of him. Elena's cheeks suddenly glowed red at the memory of the night before.

"And she will never come here?" Elena asked, looking at me keenly.

I hastened to reassure her. She paused and started to take my hand in her burning fingers, but immediately pushed it away as if coming to her senses.

"It can't be that she really finds me disgusting," I thought. "She's just being cautious, or... or perhaps the poor child has been so badly mistreated that she's afraid to trust anyone in the world."

At the appointed time, I went to fetch the medicine and stopped in at a restaurant where I was well known and could pay on credit. I had brought with me a small pot from home and had the restaurant fill it with chicken soup for Elena. But she refused to eat any, so I left the soup warming on the stove.

After giving her the medicine, I sat down to work. I thought she was asleep, but inadvertently glanced over and saw that she had raised her head and was watching me intently as I wrote. I pretended not to notice her.

Finally, Elena did fall asleep and, to my great delight, slept quietly without delirium and without groans. I was suddenly struck by the thought that Natasha, unaware of what was happening with Elena, might be very angry with me for not coming to see her that day. She might be doubly disappointed by my lack of attention at a time when she seemed to need me most, to have something important to tell me. My failure to show up could appear to her to be a deliberate snub.

As for Anna Andreyevna, I had no idea what excuse I could give for arriving a day late. I thought and thought and then suddenly decided to run to see both of them. I would only be absent about two hours and Elena was asleep and would not hear me go. I jumped up, threw on my coat, grabbed my cap, and was about to leave, when Elena suddenly called to me. I wondered instantly if she had only been pretending to be asleep.

I should point out that even though Elena's outward behavior clearly demonstrated that she did not want to talk with me, her regular need to make contact with me demonstrated quite the opposite objective and, I confess, I found this reassuring.

"Where are you planning to send me?" she asked as I approached her. In general, her infrequent questions came so unexpectedly that I was never prepared for them. This time it took a moment for me to understand what she was asking.

"Just now you were talking with your friend about sending me to work in some house. I don't want to go."

I bent down and could feel the heat emanating from her. She was once again burning with fever. I tried to comfort and assure her that if she wanted to stay with me, I wouldn't send her anywhere. As I said this, I took off my coat and cap. I wasn't going to leave her alone in her present condition.

"No, go!" she said, immediately sensing that I was planning to stay. "I'm tired. I need to sleep. I promise I'll go to sleep right away."

"But how will you get along alone?" I asked, uncertainly. "Although I shouldn't be gone for more than two hours."

"Well, go then. What'll happen if I'm sick for a year? You can't just sit around the house staring at me." She tried to smile and looked at me strangely, as though struggling with some sympathetic feeling stirring in her heart. Poor little thing! Her gentle, tender heart was revealing itself in spite of her remoteness and evident mistrust.

I decided to run to Anna Andreyevna first. She was waiting for me with great impatience and reproached me right away; she was terribly anxious. Nikolai Sergeich had gone out immediately after dinner and she had no idea where he was. I sensed that the old woman would not be able to resist telling him everything, as usual, in tiny little hints. She couldn't help it, she admitted, wanting to share her joy with him, but Nikolai Sergeich was, in her own words, blacker than the storm clouds. "He says nothing. Won't answer my questions. And suddenly after dinner, he just gets up and walks out."

As she told me this, she was practically trembling with fear and begged me to wait with her until Nikolai Sergeich returned. I pleaded and told her flat out that I would come the next day. I had, in fact, run there precisely to tell her just that. This time we almost quarreled. She cried and sharply and bitterly reproached me, and only when I started for the door did she suddenly throw herself on my neck, hug me with both arms, and tell me that she wasn't angry with her "little orphan," and that I shouldn't take offense at her words.

Natasha, contrary to my expectations, did not seem as happy to see me as she had been the day before and on other occasions. It was as if I were, in some way, intruding on her. When I asked her if Alyosha had been there that day, she replied, "Of course he was, but he only stayed a short time. He promised to look in on me tonight," she added, distractedly.

"And was he here last night, too?"

"N-no! He was detained!" she added quickly. "Well, Vanya, how are things going with you?"

I saw that for some reason she wanted to end the conversation and turn to another subject. I looked at her closely. She was obviously upset. When she saw that I was studying her closely, she suddenly grew angry and looked at me with such force that her eyes seemed to burn into me. "She's very unhappy about something," I thought, "but she does *not* want to talk about it with me."

In response to her question about my work, I told her about Elena, leaving out none of the details. She seemed extremely interested and even impressed with my story.

"Oh, my God!" she cried. "And you left her all alone... sick!"

I explained to Natasha that I hadn't planned on coming to see her at all that day, but that I was afraid she was angry with me and needed me for something.

"Need you," she said to herself, thinking about something. "Perhaps I do need you, Vanya, but it will have to wait until next time. Have you been to see my family?"

I told her about my visit with her mother.

"Yes, God knows how my father will react to this latest development. And yet, what is there to react to?"

"What do you mean, 'what is there to react to?'" I asked. "A crisis like this?"

"Yes, so... Where do you suppose he went this time? The last time this happened, you thought he came to see *me*. Look, Vanya, if you can, come see me tomorrow. Maybe I'll have something to tell you then. I'm so ashamed to have to bother you. But now you should get home to your guest. I suppose it's been a couple of hours since you left her?"

"Yes, about that. Good-bye, Natasha. But what happened with you and Alyosha today?"

"What? Alyosha? Oh, nothing. I'm surprised you're so curious."

"Good-bye, my friend."

"Good-bye." She gave me her hand clumsily and turned away to avoid my final farewell glance. I left feeling quite puzzled. "And yet," I thought, "she has a lot on her mind. It's no laughing matter. By tomorrow she'll be anxious to tell me everything."

I returned home, depressed, and was shocked when I walked through my door. It was already dark. I could see Elena sitting on the sofa with her head on her chest, as if deep in thought. She didn't look up at me, but as I approached her, I heard her mumble something. "I wonder if she's delirious?" I thought.

"Elena, my dear, what's the matter?" I asked, sitting down beside her and covering her hand with mine.

"I want to go... I'd rather be with her," she said, without raising her head to me.

"Where? To whom?" I asked in surprise.

"To her... Bubnova. She says that I owe her a lot of money because she paid to have Mama buried. I don't want her to say nasty things about Mama. I want to work for her and pay her back what I owe. Then, I can leave on my own. I'm going back to her."

"Elena," I said, "Calm down. You can't go back to her. She'll torment you. She'll destroy you!"

"Let her destroy me, let her torment me!" Elena repeated my words excitedly. "I won't be the first. Others, much better than me, have suffered. There was a beggar woman on the street who told me I was poor and that I wanted to be poor. All my life, I'll be poor.

My mother told me *that* when she was dying. I'm going to work... I don't want to wear this dress..."

"I'll buy you another one tomorrow. And I'll bring you your books, too. You'll live with me. I won't let anyone take you away from me if you don't want to go. Take it easy..."

"I'll be a servant girl!"

"All right, all right! Just relax now. Lie down and go to sleep!"

But the poor child burst into tears. Little by little, her tears turned to sobs. I didn't know what to do, so I brought her water and dabbed her temples, her forehead. Finally, she fell back on the sofa in complete exhaustion and began to shiver again with feverish chills. I wrapped her up in whatever I could find and she fell into a restless sleep, constantly trembling and waking up frequently. I'd had an exhausting day and was determined to go to bed as soon as possible. Dreadful thoughts consumed my brain. I sensed that I would have a lot of trouble with this girl, but I was more concerned about Natasha and *her* situation. As I look back on that moment, I realize that I've rarely been as depressed as I was when I fell asleep on that unfortunate night.

CHAPTER TWENTY-FOUR

I woke up late, about ten o'clock in the morning, feeling dreadful. My head was spinning and I had a terrible headache. I looked at Elena's bed and saw that it was empty. At the same moment, I heard a sound from the other room of someone sweeping the floor with a broom. I went to look. Elena was standing there holding a broom in one hand and holding up the hem of her elegant dress (which she had not yet removed from the evening before) to keep it from dragging on the dirty floor. There was firewood for the stove piled in a corner, the table had been cleared, and the kettle scrubbed. Simply put, Elena was doing the housework.

"Look, Elena," I called to her, "who asked you to clean the floor? I don't want you making yourself sicker than you already are. Do you think I brought you here to be my housemaid?"

"Who's going to tidy up, then?" she said, straightening up and looking at me haughtily. "I'm not sick now."

"But I didn't bring you here to work, Elena. Are you afraid that I might reproach you like Madame Bubnova; that you have to repay me for letting you live here? And where did you get that disgusting broom? I don't have a broom," I added, looking at her in surprise.

"This is my broom. I brought it here myself. I used to clean up for Grandpa. The broom has been here, under the stove, right where I left it."

I returned to the other room, deep in thought. Was I wrong to think that she could accept my hospitality without doing something to repay me, to avoid being in my debt? Did my kindness make her resentful? Two minutes later she came in and sat down on the couch and stared at me in silence, just as she had the evening before. Meanwhile, I boiled water in the kettle and made tea, poured her a cup, and handed it to her with a piece of white bread. She ate in silence and without comment. She hadn't eaten anything in nearly twenty-four hours.

"You've stained your nice dress with that filthy broom," I said, noticing the big dirty band at the hem of her skirt.

She looked around and suddenly, to my great surprise, put down her teacup, grabbed the front of her muslin dress in both hands and ripped it open in one pull from top to bottom. As the cloth settled around her waist, she looked up at me silently with a cold, hard expression. Her face was pale.

"What are you doing, Elena?" I cried, thinking that she had suddenly gone insane.

"This is an evil dress," she said, almost breathless with excitement. "Why do you call this a nice dress? I don't want to wear it!" She suddenly jumped up, letting the torn garment fall to the floor. She was now wearing only her undergarment. "I didn't want it. She forced me to wear it for that man. I already tore one dress, ripped it to shreds. Tore it! Ripped it!"

She then reached down and grabbed it off the floor, tearing furiously at the unfortunate dress. In a moment there remained little more than tattered strips of cloth. When she finished, she was pale white and so agitated that she could hardly stand still. I was surprised to see such bitterness. She looked at me with a defiant scowl, as if I were guilty of something too. But I already knew what I had to do.

I would go immediately, that morning, to buy her a new dress. This wild, fierce creature could only be tamed in one way: through kindness. She looked to me like someone who had never known even a single kind person. In spite of having been severely punished for tearing one dress, she had done it again with even greater ferocity this time, as if recalling the terrible memory of that earlier event.

In Tolkutchy Market, one could buy a plain, simple dress for very little money. Unfortunately, at that moment, I had almost no money at all. I had decided the night before that I would go in the morning to a place near Tolkutchy where I could get some money. I grabbed my cap. As I headed toward the door, Elena followed me with her eyes, as if waiting for something.

"Are you going to lock me in?" she asked, as I picked up the key to my apartment door, just as I had done the night before and on every other occasion when I went out.

"My dear friend," I said, walking up to her. "Don't be upset with me for that. I lock my door because someone might try to get in. You're sick and I don't want you to be frightened. Who knows? Bubnova herself might take it into her head to come here..."

I told her this quite deliberately. I really was locking the door because I didn't trust her. It seemed to me that she might suddenly decide to run away from me at any time. Until she could convince me otherwise, I decided to be cautious. Elena said nothing and I locked her in again.

I knew an entrepreneur who had recently published the third volume of a multi-volume compilation of articles. He occasionally gave me work and paid regularly. I went to him and managed to get an advance of twenty-five rubles upon my promise to deliver a new article to him within a week. I had been hoping to find some time to work on my novel, but he was a reliable resource if I wanted to avoid complete destitution.

Having obtained the money, I went to Tolkutchy. There I soon found a familiar old peddler woman who sold old clothes. I pantomimed Elena's size and she instantly found for me a simple dress made of a light-colored cotton, very strong and only washed once, for a very low price. I also took a kerchief for Elena's neck and as I was paying, I realized that Elena would need a coat or shawl or something like that. The weather was cold and she had absolutely nothing. But I put off that purchase for another day. Elena was so sensitive and proud. God alone knew how she was going to react to the dress, despite the fact that I had deliberately chosen one as simple and unpretentious as possible. Nevertheless, I still bought her two pairs of cotton stockings and one pair of woolen. I would give them to her on the pretext that she was sick and the room was cold. She would also need new undergarments, but I decided to hold off until Elena was more comfortable with me. I also bought some inexpensive curtains for the bed, something I thought was necessary under the circumstances, and I hoped would give her a little pleasure.

I returned home with my purchases around one o'clock. I had unlocked the door as inaudibly as possible, so Elena did not realize I had returned. She was standing at the table looking through my books and papers but when she heard me she quickly shut the book she was reading and walked away from the table, blushing. I looked at the book and discovered that it was my first novel, published in book form, and on the title page of which was printed my name.

"Do you always break in on someone without knocking," she said in a teasing tone. "Someone came by while you were gone but the door was locked."

"It might have been the doctor," I said. "Did you call out to him?"

"No."

I said nothing but took the bundle, untied it and took out the dress.

"Here, my dear Elena," I said, approaching her, "you can't go out dressed in those rags. I bought you a dress. It's very simple and the cheapest one I could find, so you have nothing to worry about. It was just one ruble twenty kopecks. Wear it in good health."

I put the dress beside her. She blushed and looked at me with wide eyes. She was extremely surprised, and a little ashamed, I thought. There was something soft and gentle in her eyes that lit up her face. When she said nothing, I turned back to the table. My act of kindness seemed to have moved her, but her willpower prevailed and she sat down without taking her eyes off the floor.

My head still ached and was spinning more and more. The fresh air had not brought me the slightest relief. Meanwhile, I had to go to Natasha. My concern about her had not decreased since the previous day. On the contrary, it had grown more and more. Suddenly, I had a feeling that Elena wanted to say something to me and turned to her.

"When you leave, don't lock me in," she said, looking away and moving her finger along a seam on the armrest of the couch as if completely fascinated by its stitching. "I have nowhere else to go."

"Well, Elena, I agree. But if a stranger comes? Perhaps... God knows who."

"So leave me the key and I'll lock the door from inside. And if someone knocks, I'll just call out, "There's no one home!" And she looked at me with a shrug that seemed to say, "That's how easy it is!"

Before I could respond, she suddenly asked, "Who washes your clothes?"

"There is a woman, here in this house."

"I know how to wash clothes. Where did you get that food you brought me yesterday?"

"At the inn."

"I know how to cook. I'll cook for you."

"Come on now, Elena, what do you know about cooking? Let's not discuss it."

Elena paused and looked down. She seemed quite upset by my comment. At least ten minutes went by before she spoke again.

"Soup," she said suddenly, without looking up.

"What about soup? What kind of soup?" I asked, surprised.

"I know how to cook soup. I made soup for Mama when she was sick. I even went to the market."

"Elena, you're very proud," I said, going to her and sitting next to her on the couch. "I understand how you feel. I understand in my heart. You're all alone now, without family, unhappy. I want to help you. You'd do the same for me, if I were sick. But you won't admit that, so it's hard for you to accept my gift of friendship. You immediately want to pay me back because you're afraid I'll be angry, like Bubnova. If that is what you're feeling, you don't have to be embarrassed, Elena."

She did not answer, but her lips were quivering. It seemed that she wanted to tell me something, but she refrained and kept silent. I got up to go to Natasha. This time I left the key for Elena. "Lock the door when I leave," I told her. "And if anyone knocks, be sure to call out, 'Who is it?'"

I was absolutely convinced that something bad had happened to Natasha and that she was keeping it from me, as she had often done in the past. At any rate, I was determined to stay for only a moment so as not to annoy her with my insistence.

And that's exactly what happened. She once again met me with that same hard, unhappy look. I wanted to retreat immediately, but my legs gave way.

"I just came to see you for a minute, Natasha," I said. "For advice. What should I do about my guest?" I quickly began to tell her more about Elena. Natasha listened to me silently.

"I don't know what to suggest, Vanya," she answered. "From what you've told me, I'd say she's a very strange creature. Maybe she's been hurt, scared. Give her a little time to recover. Are you thinking of her living with my family?"

"She says she won't leave me. And God knows what it would be like with your parents, so I don't know. But tell me, my dear friend, how are you? Yesterday, you didn't seem at all well," I said timidly.

"Yes. I still have something of a headache today," she answered absently. "Have you been to see my folks?"

"No. Tomorrow I'll go. After all, tomorrow is Saturday."

"What has that got to do with anything?"

"The prince is coming in the evening."

"So what? I haven't forgotten."

"No, I was just..."

She stood in front of me for a long time staring at me. In her eyes was a kind of determination, a doggedness; something intense, feverish.

"You know what, Vanya," she said. "Be kind enough to leave me. You're really disturbing me."

I rose from my chair, unable to hide my look of inexpressible astonishment.

"My dear, Natasha! What is it? What's happened?" I cried in fright.

"Nothing has happened! All... you will know all tomorrow, but for now I want to be alone. Listen, Vanya, leave now. It's so hard... so hard to look at you!"

"But tell me at least..."

"Tomorrow! All will be known tomorrow! Oh, my God! Please, go away!"

I went out. I was so disturbed that I barely knew where I was going. Mavra ran down the hall after me.

"Why is she so angry?" she asked me. "I'm afraid to go anywhere near her."

"But what's the matter with her?" I asked.

"It's been three days since he last showed his face here."

"Three days?" I asked in amazement. "But she told me just yesterday that Alyosha was here yesterday morning, and that she was expecting him last night."

"Last night? No. And he wasn't here in the morning either! I tell you, we haven't laid eyes on him in three days. Did she really tell you he was here yesterday morning?"

"That's what she told me."

"Well," Mavra said, deep in thought, "she must really be hurting if she won't even admit it to *you*. A fine gentleman *he* is!"

"What does it all mean?" I cried.

"The truth is I don't know what to do with her," Mavra cried, waving her hands. "Yesterday, she started to send me to fetch him, but twice stopped me on the street and made me return. And today she won't say a word to me. I wish you would go to see him. I don't dare leave her alone."

I rushed outside and down the stairs.

"We'll see you this evening, won't we?" Mavra shouted after me.

"We shall see," I called back to her. "I may just run up to ask you how she is! If I'm still alive!"

I really felt as if I had been struck in the heart.

CHAPTER TWENTY-FIVE

I went straight to Alyosha. He lived with his father on Malaya Morskaya near Saint Isaac's Square. The prince had a very large apartment, despite the fact that he usually lived alone. Alyosha was currently occupying two beautifully furnished rooms. I very rarely visited him there. In fact, this would be only my second visit. He came to see *me* more often, especially at first, during the early stages of his courtship of Natasha.

He was not at home. I went straight up to his rooms and wrote him the following note:

"Alyosha, you seem to have gone completely mad. Considering that on Tuesday evening your father personally asked Natasha to do you the honor of being your wife, and you were glad to have this request (which I witnessed) made for you, you must admit that your behavior in this situation is somewhat strange. Do you know what you're doing to Natasha? I write to remind you that your conduct toward your future wife has been unworthy of you and frivolous to the highest degree. I know very well that I have no right to preach to you, but I choose to disregard that fact.

"P. S. Natasha knows nothing about this letter and she was not the one who told me about you."

I folded the note and left it on the table. When I spoke to the servant I was told that Alexey was hardly ever at home and that he wasn't expected back until nearly dawn.

I went straight home. My head was swimming and my legs were weak and trembling. The door was already unlocked. As I entered, I saw Nikolai Sergeich Ichmenyev waiting for me. He was sitting at the table in silence, staring in amazement at Elena, who was sitting on the couch and staring back at him with an expression of equal surprise, although stubbornly silent. "It's clear," I thought, "that she must seem very strange to him."

"Ah, my friend," the old man said, "I have been waiting an hour for you and, frankly, did not expect... to find you living like..."

He looked around the room, seemingly paying no mind to Elena. I could see his astonishment clearly reflected in his eyes. But looking at him closer, he also appeared apprehensive and depressed. His face was paler than usual.

"Sit down, sit down," he continued, with an anxious wave of his hand. "I hurried here to see you but... but what's wrong with you? You look terrible."

"I'm not feeling at all well. I've felt dizzy since this morning."

"Well, look, that's not something you should ignore. Have you a cold or what?"

"No, it's just a kind of nervous condition. I have it sometimes. But what about you? Is there something troubling you?"

"No, nothing, nothing! There is the lawsuit, of course. Sit down."

I pulled up a chair and sat facing him at the table. The old man leaned slightly toward me and whispered.

"Now don't look at her and pretend we're talking about something else. What have you got to say about this little visitor of yours?"

"I'll tell you all about her later," I said. "This poor girl, a complete orphan, is the granddaughter of the very Smith who lived here and died outside of the pastry shop."

"Ah, so it's his granddaughter! Well, brother, she's a bit peculiar, isn't she? See how she just stares at me? If you hadn't shown up in the next five minutes, I would have left! It took forever to convince her to unlock the door and she hasn't said a word since 'Who is it?' Why is she here? I supposed she came to see her grandfather, not knowing he was dead?"

"Yes. She was devastated when I told her. When the old man died, his last few words were about her."

"Hmmm! The grandfather sounds a lot like the granddaughter. But you can tell me more about them both later. If she's as poor as you say, maybe we can do something to help her out a little. But for now, do you think you can send her on her way? I've got some serious matters to discuss with you."

"No, I can't send her away. She lives here... with me. She has no one else in the world. But you're free to talk in front of her. After all, she's just a child and, as you can see, she doesn't talk much."

"Well, yes, of course, a child. But I'm really quite stunned. You say she's living with you? Good God in heaven!"

The old man looked at her in amazement again. Elena, sensing that we were talking about her, sat silently, her head down and her fingers once again following the stitches on the armrest of the sofa. She was wearing her new dress, which fit her perfectly, and her hair was neatly combed, perhaps in honor of the dress. Truth be told, were it not for the strange, wild look in her eyes, she would have appeared to be a perfectly lovely young girl.

"Short and sweet, that's what I have to tell you, brother," the old man began again. "It's very complicated, a most important matter..."

He sat with downcast eyes that clearly reflected the importance of his message, but in spite of his haste and his promise of "short and sweet," he couldn't seem to find the words to begin. "I wonder what's happened," I thought.

"You see, Vanya, I've come to ask you for a favor. But first... I should probably explain to you the circumstances... extremely delicate circumstances..."

He cleared his throat and stole a glance at me, then looked away and blushed, red-faced with rage at his own awkwardness. He was angry but resolved to continue.

"Well, how should I put this? It's really quite simple. I plan to challenge the prince to a duel and would like you to arrange the matter and be my second."

I fell back in my chair and stared at him in amazement.

"Why do you look at me like that?" he asked. "I'm not crazy."

"But, excuse me, Nikolai Sergeich, what reason... on what pretext? And, ultimately, why would you want to?"

"Pretext! Reason!" the old man cried. "That's rich!"

"All right, all right, I know what you're going to say, but how can this help your situation? What could you possibly gain from a duel? I confess, I don't understand."

"I didn't suppose you *would* understand. Listen, son, our lawsuit is over, or practically. There are just one or two formalities to take care of. I've lost. The Court says I have to pay him ten thousand rubles. And Ichmenyevka is all I have for security. So this vile man, who has all the money he needs, takes title to Ichmenyevka, I'm all paid up, and once again I'm a free man. I'll be able to hold my head up and say to this... so and so... this *worthy* prince, 'You have insulted me for the past two years. You've disgraced my name and the honor of my family and I've had to endure all of this! You wouldn't allow me to challenge you to a duel before this because you told me outright, "You're a clever man, you want to kill me so you won't have to pay me the money you know will be awarded to me sooner or later! No, first let's see how the litigation is resolved and we'll see." Well now, my dear Prince, the case is resolved, you have my land, so there is no longer any barrier to our meeting on the field of honor. What, did you imagine that I wouldn't want to avenge myself eventually for everything, for everything you did to me?'"

His eyes sparkled. I stared at him in silence. I tried to probe his secret thoughts.

"Listen, Nikolai Sergeich," I finally said, determined to tell him what had to be said, the key point, without which we could not understand each other. "May I be totally honest with you?"

"You may," he answered firmly.

"Tell me straight. Is this idea of yours prompted solely by your desire for revenge or have you another objective in mind?"

"Ivan Petrovich," he answered, "you know that I do not discuss certain matters in conversation, matters that I keep close to the vest, so to speak. But I will make an exception with you this one time, because you have a clear, sharp mind and have at once seen through my plan. Yes, I have another purpose. My objective is to save my lost daughter and to steer her away from the path to destruction that past circumstances have now led her to."

"But how can you save Natasha by dueling with the prince, that's my question?"

"To stop in its tracks a plot that is now afoot. Listen. Do not imagine for one second that this is all sparked by some kind of paternal affection or similar weakness. All that is nonsense! I do not reveal the inside of my heart to anyone. Not even to you. My daughter deserted me, walked out of my house with her lover, and on that night I cast her out of my life, tore her from my heart forever, you remember? Just because you saw me sobbing over her portrait does not mean that I am willing to forgive her. I do not forgive her. I wept for lost happiness, for a vanquished dream, but not about her, as she is today. I may, on occasion, but not often, cry, and I'm not ashamed to admit it, just as I am not ashamed to admit that until that day I loved my daughter more than anything else on Earth. All of this may seem to contradict my current outburst. You may ask, if I am so indifferent to the fate of someone I no longer consider my daughter, why am I so concerned with thwarting a plot to lead her astray? I answer: first, I do not want to see that loathsome, treacherous man triumph in any way and, secondly, from the most basic feelings of humanity. Even if she is no longer my daughter, she is still a weak, insecure and easily deceived creature who does not deserve to be utterly destroyed. I cannot get involved in this matter directly, but indirectly, by way of a duel, I can. If he kills me or sheds my blood, do you think she would step over my dead body and stand before the altar with my murderer's son, as cruelly, say, as the daughter of Servius Tullius—remember that book I gave you from which you learned to read? —when she drove a chariot over the corpse of her father? And finally, if I should come out victorious, the other princes will certainly not permit the wedding to go forward. In short, I do not want this marriage and I will do anything in my power to prevent it. Do you understand me now?"

"No. If you wish to honor Natasha, how can you interfere with her marriage, which is exactly what is needed to restore her good name? After all, if she is to live happily on Earth for many years, she needs her good name."

"She can spit on the opinion of these contemptible people! Do you think I care what *they* think of me or of her? The greatest shame of all would be for her to enter into such a marriage, to be attached in any way to that despicable crowd. A noble pride, that is the answer to a disdainful world. Then, maybe then, I would be willing to extend my hand to her, and woe to anyone who dares to dishonor my daughter!"

Such a desperate and naïve idealism amazed me. But I quickly realized that he was speaking out of anger and had not yet considered the full impact of what he was proposing.

"You're asking too much of her," I said, "callously demanding a strength from her, a force, which you did not provide for her at birth. Do you think she has agreed to the marriage because she wants to be a princess? No, she is in love, it's passion, it's fate. And finally, you have so much contempt for public opinion and yet you bow down before it yourself. The prince has offended you; you have been publicly accused of trying to marry your daughter into a princely house through fraud and deceit, and here you are, reasoning that if she refuses the marriage *now*, after a formal proposal on their part, then, of course, this will be the most thorough and obvious refutation of the old slander. That is what you are hoping for. And yet you will only feed his low opinion of you by trying to force him to confess his mistake. You want to make him appear foolish and for that you would sacrifice the happiness of your daughter. All to satisfy your own ego!"

The old man frowned and did not speak for a while.

"You're being unfair to me, Vanya," he said to me at last, and tears shone on his eyelashes. "I swear to you, unfair. But let's leave it! I cannot turn my heart inside out for you." He stood and picked up his hat. "One thing I will say. You have been talking about the happiness of my daughter. I absolutely and unquestionably do not believe that this will be a happy marriage. And more than that, without my intervention, this marriage will never take place."

"What do you mean? Why do say that? Do you know something you haven't told me?" I asked anxiously.

"No, I don't know anything special. But that damned fox could never have decided on such a path. It's all nonsense, some kind of trap. I'm sure of that, and mark my words, the truth will come out. Second, if the marriage actually does take place, it will happen only because that scoundrel has some mysterious, secret plan by which this marriage will benefit him in some way, some financial advantage which I do not yet understand. And finally, decide for yourself. Can you honestly say, from your heart, that she will be happy in this marriage? There will be reproaches, humiliations, from a foolish boy who is already tiring of her love, and who, once the vows have been exchanged, will begin to disrespect her, hurt and humiliate her. As her passion for him grows stronger, his for her will begin to cool, the result being jealousy, pain, living hell, a divorce, maybe even crime itself. No, Vanya! If you are still assisting them to make this happen, I predict that you will have to answer to God, but it will be too late! Good-bye!"

I stopped him.

"Listen, Nikolai Sergeich, we can work this out. Be patient. Be assured that there are more than one pair of eyes watching this unfold, and maybe it can be resolved in the best way possible, on its own, without the intervention of force or artificial means, such as this duel. Time is the best peacemaker! And finally, let me tell you that your entire scheme is completely impossible. Surely you can't believe for one minute that Prince Valkovsky will accept your challenge?"

"Not accept? Why do you say that?"

"I swear to you, he will not accept. And believe me when I say that he will find some perfectly legitimate excuse, something that will make him appear dignified and stately, while you will be completely ridiculed..."

"My boy, have mercy! You have wounded me with that! But how can he refuse? No, Vanya, you're just a poet, a romantic! Do you imagine that it would be indecent for him to fight me? I'm as good a man as he is. I am an old man, an injured father, and you are a Russian writer, and therefore also a respectable person who can serve as my second and... and... I really don't understand why you still need more..."

"You'll see. He will make some excuse and you will discover for yourself that your entire plan is impossible."

"Hmm... well, my friend, we'll try it your way. I will wait a respectable amount of time, of course. We'll see what time alone can do. But there's one thing more, Vanya. You must give me your word of honor that you'll never repeat a word of this conversation to anyone, especially Anna Andreyevna!"

"Of course."

"And one more favor, Vanya. Let *us* not ever talk about this matter again either."

"All right, I give you my word."

"And finally, please, I know that you probably find your visits boring, but do come by and see us more often, if you can. My poor Anna Andreyevna loves you so... and... she becomes so miserable without you... do you understand, Vanya?"

He squeezed my hand.

"I heartily promise to visit more often," I said.

"And now, Vanya, one last, delicate matter. Have you any money?"

"Money?" I repeated in amazement.

"Yes." The old man blushed and lowered his eyes. "I look around at your apartment... at your circumstances... and when I think that you must now have other... extra expenses..." He nodded toward Elena and reached into his pocket. "Here, my boy, one hundred and fifty rubles for a first installment."

"One hundred and fifty! A first installment! But you've just lost your lawsuit!"

"Vanya, you really don't understand, do you? You may have some urgent need in the future. Or you can use the money to help you make an independent decision, free from outside influence. Perhaps you don't need it now, but with the Mademoiselle... there may be a time in the future... Anyway, I'll leave it with you. That's all I could come up with. If you don't spend it, you can always return it. But for now, farewell! My God, how pale you are! You look terrible..."

I did not argue and took the money. It was all too clear why he left it with me.

"I can hardly stand on my feet," I answered him.

"Do not ignore it, Vanya, my boy, take care of yourself! Do not go out today. I will tell Anna Andreyevna about your condition. Do you need a doctor? I'll visit again tomorrow; at least I'll try, if my legs will carry me. Now, you should lie down. Well, good-bye. Good-bye, little girl. Look, see how she turns her back on me?" He spoke quietly in my ear. "Listen, my friend, here are five more rubles, for the girl. But you mustn't say I left them for her. Just buy her something. Get her some new shoes, underwear... she'll need a lot of things. Farewell, my friend!"

I accompanied him to the gate. After he left, I asked the porter to fetch some food at the inn. Elena had not had lunch.

CHAPTER TWENTY-SIX

But as soon as I returned upstairs I felt dizzy and collapsed in the middle of the room. I remember Elena screaming and rushing to grab me before I hit the floor. I remember nothing after that.

When I awoke, I found myself already in bed. Elena told me later that she, along with the porter who had brought her lunch, had moved me there. I woke up several times and each time I saw Elena's sweet, caring face staring down at me. But all of that I remember as if in a dream, obscured by a dense fog, the sweet image of a lovely young girl appearing in flashes out of the haze like a vision. She brought me things to drink and sat beside me on the bed with a sad, frightened look, running her soft, tiny fingers through my hair. One time, I remember her gentle kiss on my face. On another occasion, waking suddenly in the night with just the light of a candle standing on the table next to the bed, I saw the silhouette of Elena's face lying next to me on the pillow. She was sleeping quietly, her pale lips half parted, with one hand cupped under her cheek. It wasn't until the following morning that I was fully conscious. The candle had burned down to a small puddle of wax and the bright pink rays of dawn were already playing on the wall. Elena was sitting in a chair next to the table, her head bowed low and her chin resting on her left hand. She was fast asleep. I remember gazing a long time at her sweet, innocent face, which even in dreams bore a sad, unchildlike expression and a strange, deathly beauty, pale, with long lashes on thin cheeks, framed by jet-black hair, thick and flowing, tied carelessly on the side. Her other hand lay on my pillow. I softly kissed her thin little hand and even though the child was not awake, I thought I caught the glimmer of a smile dance on her pale lips. I continued looking at her until, finally, I drifted quietly into a deep, healing sleep. This time, I slept until almost noon. Waking up, I felt almost fully recovered. Only a general weakness and a heaviness in my limbs bore witness to my recent illness. I had had similar nervous attacks before and I had grown used to them. The illness rarely lasted more than a day, but inflicted mayhem on my mind and body before subsiding into oblivion.

It was almost noon. The first thing I noticed was a heavy string stretched across one corner of the room. The curtains I had purchased the day before were attached and partially hid the sofa, which Elena had pushed into the corner, providing herself with a small private bedroom of her own.

She was sitting before the stove boiling the kettle. When she saw that I was awake, she smiled cheerfully and immediately came over to me.

"My dear friend," I said, taking her hand, "You have been up all night looking after me. I didn't know you could be so caring."

"And how do you know that I was looking after you? Maybe I just went to bed and slept through the night," she said, looking at me with a sly, good-natured playfulness, but at the same time blushing shyly at her own words.

"I woke up and saw everything. You fell asleep just before dawn."

"Would you like some tea?" she interrupted, as if having difficulty continuing this line of conversation, a trait all too common among modest, open-hearted people who are uncomfortable accepting praise.

"I would love some," I answered. "But did you ever get anything to eat yesterday?"

"I didn't have supper, but I did have a late lunch. The porter brought it. You, however, should not be speaking. Get some rest. You're still not completely well."

She brought me my tea and sat down next to me on the bed.

"Rest, I will… for now," I told her. "But before nightfall, I must get up and go see someone. I really have to, my little darling."

"Oh, is that right? Who do you have to see? Was it that man who was here yesterday?"

"No, not him."

"That's good, I didn't like him. He's the one who got you all upset yesterday. To see his daughter, then?"

"And what do you know about his daughter?"

"I heard everything yesterday," she said, looking down at me, her face darkening and her eyebrows shifting down over her eyes. "He's a horrible old man," she added.

"You don't know anything about him. He's actually a very good man."

"No, no, he was nasty! I heard him," she said with fervor.

"What did you hear?"

"He refuses to forgive his daughter..."

"But he loves her. She behaved very badly towards him, and yet he feels tormented because he's so worried about her."

"Why doesn't he just forgive her then? But even if he did forgive his daughter, she shouldn't come back to him."

"But why? Why shouldn't she?"

"Because he doesn't deserve her kindness," she answered eagerly. "She should stay away and become a beggar on the streets, and then let him *see* her begging on the streets and that will make him suffer even more."

Her eyes sparkled and her cheeks glowed.

She may actually be right, I thought to myself.

"Was he the man whose home you wanted to send me to?" she added after a moment.

"Yes, Elena."

"No, I'd rather take a job as a servant."

"Oh, but that doesn't make any sense, my darling. It's silly. Who would hire you as a servant?"

"Any man," she answered quickly, looking more and more downcast. She was visibly irritated.

"Yes, but what peasant or working man is going to hire a girl like you as a servant?" I asked, grinning.

"Well, then a nobleman."

"A girl with your temperament living in the home of a nobleman?"

"I can change!" The more annoyed she became, the more snappish were her replies.

"Maybe, but you couldn't stand to be mistreated."

"I can! They could scold me all they want, I would purposely remain silent. They could beat me, I would be silent, completely silent, even *as* they were beating me. And I wouldn't cry. That would annoy them even more if I didn't cry."

"What happened to you, Elena? To be so angry, and yet so proud? You must have known so much unhappiness."

I got up and walked over to my dining table. Elena stayed on the couch, gazing distractedly at the armrest, her fingers scratching at the stitching. She said nothing.

"She's probably mad at me for what I said," I thought.

Standing at the table, I automatically opened the book I had brought home the day before to research my article, and little by little I started reading. That's often the case with me. I open up a book to check on something and before I know it I'm engrossed in reading.

"What do you write about?" Elena said, with a timid smile, as she quietly approached the table.

"Oh, all sorts of things. That's how I earn my money."

"Solicitations?"

"No, not solicitations. They're short articles about a lot of different things. But I also write stories about different people and places. And sometimes I put them all together into what is called a novel." She listened with great curiosity.

"Is it all true, what you write?"

"Well, no, I make up most of it."

"Why would you make up things that aren't true?"

"Because people like to read it. Here, you were looking at this yesterday. Do you know how to read?"

"I know how."

"Well then, see for yourself. I wrote this book."

"You? I'll read it."

There was clearly something she wanted to say, but was having difficulty getting it out. Was there some hidden message behind her questions?

"Do you get paid a lot for what you write?" she finally asked.

"Well, it depends. Sometimes a lot, and sometimes nothing at all, because the end result doesn't come out right. Writing is very hard work, Elena."

"So you're not rich?"

"No. No, I'm not rich."

"So I will work and help you."

She stared at me and then lowered her eyes and blushed. Suddenly, she rushed towards me in two quick steps, grabbed both of my hands and pressed her face tightly against my chest. I looked down at her in astonishment.

"I love you! I'm not proud," she said. "You said yesterday that I was proud. No, no... I'm not like that. I love you. And you're the only one who loves me!"

She began to weep and a moment later her chest was heaving with sobs with the same intensity as her anger from the day before. She fell to her knees in front of me and kissed my hands, my feet...

"You do love me!" she repeated. "You're the only one... the only one who cares about me."

She grabbed tightly around my knees with her arms. All of the emotions that she had so long suppressed had suddenly burst forth in one gigantic, irresistible impulse, and I understood how the coldness of a heart locked tightly from the world can suddenly melt, and the more tightly sealed the blockage the greater the need to break through the barrier and flow free. Elena's words cascaded forth in an inevitable rush of emotion, combining love, gratitude and affection, mixed with an astounding flood of tears.

She sobbed to the point of near hysteria. With difficulty, I pulled her to her feet and lifted her in my arms. I carried her to the sofa and sat next to her as she continued to sob, clinging to me and burying her face in my chest, as if ashamed to look at me.

Little by little the tears subsided and briefly, once or twice, she pulled back and let her eyes slide up my face, her gaze soft and timid, not quite ready to reveal everything. Finally, she blushed and smiled.

"Are you feeling any better?" I asked. "My sweet tender-hearted little child, my sweet Elena?"

"No, don't call me Elena," she whispered, once again hiding her face from me.

"Not Elena? What then?"

"Nellie."

"Nellie? Why Nellie? It's a very pretty name, so I'll call you that if that's what you want."

"That's what my mother called me. And no one else. Just her. And I would never want anyone else to call me that... Except you. I want you to call me Nellie. And I will always love you. Always."

"Such a loving and generous heart," I thought to myself. "But what you have put me through to earn the privilege of calling you Nellie. But now I know that I have won your heart forever."

"Nellie, listen," I said, as soon as she had calmed down. "You say that your mother was the only one who really loved you and no one else. Didn't your grandfather love you?"

"No, he didn't!"

"And yet you cried over him when he died. Remember? Here, on the stairs."

She thought for a moment.

"No, he didn't love me. He was an evil man." A disgusted look contorted her face.

"He wasn't entirely to blame, Nellie. He seems to have been completely out of his mind. He died like a madman. Remember, I told you how he died."

"Yes, but he only became forgetful in the last month before he died. He used to sit here all day waiting for me, and if I didn't show up, he would just sit here another day, and then a third day, without ever taking a drink or a bite to eat. He was much better before."

"What do you mean before? Before what?"

"Before my mother died."

"So you were the one who brought him food and drink then?"

"Yes, that was me."

"Where did you get them? From Madame Bubnova?"

"No, I never took anything from Bubnova," she insisted, her voice rising in volume.

"Then where did you get them if you had no money?"

Nellie paused and turned pale. She looked at me for a long, long time.

"I went into the streets and begged. When I had five kopecks, I would buy him bread and tobacco."

"And he *allowed* you to do that, Nellie? Nellie?"

"When I first started, I didn't tell him. But then, when he found out, he used to take me out himself and make me beg. I would stand on the bridge asking passers-by for coins, and he walked around nearby, watching and waiting, and when he saw someone give me a coin, he would throw himself at me and grab the money away, afraid that I might hide it from him, not save it for him."

Saying this, she smiled a sarcastic, bitter smile.

"It was when Mama died," she added, "that he started going funny in the head."

"So he must have been very fond of your mother. He didn't want to live without her."

"No, he didn't like her. He was angry and wouldn't forgive her... just like that evil old man from yesterday," she added, softly, almost in a whisper, as her face grew paler.

I shuddered. The plot of a novel suddenly flashed in my mind. This poor woman dying in a cellar at the undertaker's; her orphan daughter visiting from time to time her grandfather, a crazy, eccentric old man who had once cursed her mother and now dies in a pastry shop shortly after the death of his dog!

"Azorka was Mama's dog once," said Nellie suddenly, smiling at the remembrance. "Grandpa was very fond of Mama at first, and when Mama ran away she left Azorka with him. That's why he loved Azorka so much. But he never forgave Mama for leaving, and when the dog died, so did he." As she said this, the smile vanished from her face.

"Nellie, what did he do before?" I asked, after a brief pause.

"He used to be rich. I don't know what he did," she answered. "He had a factory. So Mama told me. At first she thought I was too young and didn't speak about him. She would just kiss me and say, 'You'll know everything when the time comes, my poor, unhappy child!' She was always calling me poor and unhappy. And at night, when she used to think I was asleep—and I was purposely pretending to be asleep—she would stand crying over me and kiss me and say 'poor, unhappy!'"

"What did your mother die from?"

"From consumption. It's been six weeks now."

"Do you remember when your grandfather was rich?"

"No, that was back before I was born. Mama even left Grandpa before I was born."

"Who was the man she left with?"

"I don't know," Nellie answered, quietly, as if thinking. "She went abroad and I was born there."

"Abroad? Where was that?"

"In Switzerland. I've traveled all over. Italy, Paris."

I was surprised.

"And do you remember any of that, Nellie?"

"I remember a lot."

"How is it you speak Russian so well?"

"Mama used to teach Russian even then. She was a Russian because her mother was Russian, and my Grandpa was an American, but also Russian. And when Mama came back to Russia a year-and-a-half ago, I learned the language properly. Mama was already sick. Then we got poorer and poorer and Mama was always crying. She spent a long time when we arrived in St. Petersburg searching for Grandpa, and she kept saying all the time that she was to blame, and she was always crying. Crying, crying! And when she learned that Grandpa was poor now, too, she cried even more. She tried to contact him and wrote letter after letter, but he never answered any of them."

"Why did your mother come back here? Just to find her father?"

"I don't know. But before that we lived very well." Nellie's eyes sparkled. "Mama and I lived alone together. She had a friend, a very nice man, like you. They had known each other before she ran away. But he died there, and Mama and I came back here."

"Was he the man your mother ran away with when she deserted your grandfather?"

"No, not with him. Mama went with another man... but he ended up leaving her."

"What was *his* name, Nellie?"

Nellie looked at me and said nothing. She undoubtedly knew the identity of the man who had deserted her mother, and who was probably her father. It was difficult for me to even dignify the scoundrel with a name.

I did not want to torment her with any more questions. She was an extraordinary little character, tough and passionate on the outside, but also emotionally bottled-up and afraid of being hurt; sweet, but also proud and inaccessible. In the short time I had known her, despite her professed love for me (a love that until then she had reserved only for her mother), Nellie had been careful not to expose her fragile emotions or unhappy past. But on that one day, in the course of several hours of anguished confession, interrupted frequently by convulsive sobs, she revealed her true feelings and provided me with a tale of such appalling remembrances that I shall never forget it, although her most important story was yet to come.

It was a terrible story, a story of an abandoned woman who survived unhappiness, exhaustion and illness only to be rejected by the one man upon whom she should have been able to depend: her own father, who not only insulted and cursed her, but cast her out into the world to endure the most excruciating humiliation and degradation. It was the story of a woman driven to despair, burdened with a fatherless child, slogging through the cold, muddy streets of Petersburg, begging for their sustenance, and then suffering a slow, agonizing death in a cold, damp basement, unaware that the father who had refused to pardon her for her sins, had come to his senses and would arrive in time to discover only a cold corpse instead of the precious little girl he had loved more than anything else in the world. It was a strange tale of mystery, of the barely comprehensible relationship between an old man and his granddaughter, who, even at so tender an age, already understood him and the things men do to guarantee smooth and secure lives for themselves. It was a grim story. One of those sad and painful stories which so often go unnoticed under the mysterious and brooding skies of St. Petersburg, but remain buried in the dark, hidden recesses of a great city, between the foolish, extravagant debaucheries of the egoists and the dull, selfish stupidity and secret criminal vices that make up the pandemonium and hell of senseless and abnormal life. But her story is not over yet.

Also Recommended

"Yellen has given us the Jewish-American immigrant experience more vitally and persuasively than any writer since Isaac Bashevis Singer."   Christopher Davis

Cousin Bella – The Whore of Minsk recounts the life of a young Jewish woman in Tsarist Russia who was sold into prostitution, rescued by the author's indomitable grandmother, and then immigrated to America where the most extraordinary drama of her life was yet to unfold. Written by Tony® nominee and two-time Emmy® winning screenwriter, Sherman Yellen. Also included is Yellen's holiday classic, *A Christmas Lilly*, a tender, poignant memory of a Jewish family's first Christmas tree in 1939, celebrating the author's wise and compassionate mother.

Trade Paperback ISBN-13: 978-1495290435 Paperback $8.95
Also Available in **Kindle eBook** and **Unabridged Audiobook**

MORECLACKE PUBLISHING

Also Recommended

The Flash of Midnight
By Robert Armin

Taking its inspiration from Voltaire's *Candide*, Robert Armin's novel *The Flash of Midnight* recounts the bisexual escapades of Laurie Norber, a young woman who steadfastly believes that true love is just around the corner, never imagining that in June of 1969 she will become the spark that ignites a sexual revolution at a Greenwich Village bar called the Stonewall Inn.

Trade Paperback ISBN-13: 978-1463508074 Paperback $12.95

Also Available in **Kindle eBook** and **Unabridged Audiobook**

MORECLACKE PUBLISHING

Also Recommended

Three new plays by two-time Emmy Award® winning *(The Adams Chronicles* and *An Early Frost)* and Tony Award® nominated *(The Rothschilds)* writer Sherman Yellen, with a Foreward by Pulitzer Prize winning lyricist Sheldon Harnick. Featuring both comic and dramatic female roles from 40 to 80 and male roles from 20 to 60.

Trade Paperback ISBN-13: 978-0996016902 Paperback $16.95

MORECLACKE **PUBLISHING**

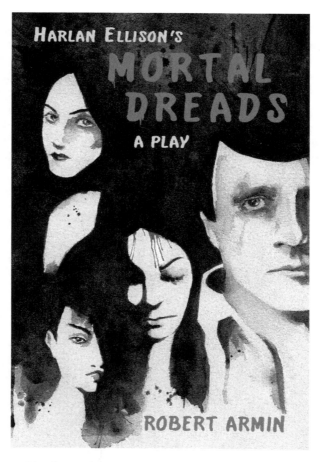

Also Recommended

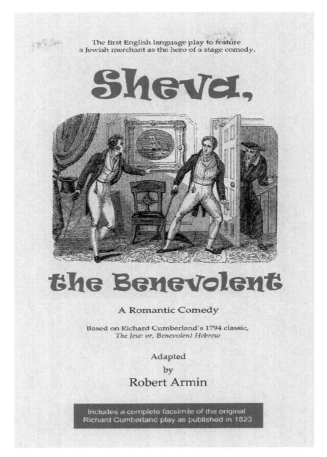

The first English language play to feature
a Jewish merchant as the hero of a stage comedy.

Sheva,

the Benevolent

A Romantic Comedy

Based on Richard Cumberland's 1794 classic,
The Jew: or, Benevolent Hebrew

Adapted
by
Robert Armin

Includes a complete facsimile of the original
Richard Cumberland play as published in 1823

Sheva, the Benevolent is a faithful adaptation of Richard Cumberland's 1794 comedy, *The Jew: or, Benevolent Hebrew*, featuring Sheva, the first Jewish moneylender to be portrayed as the hero of a stage comedy. Includes a Preface by playwright Robert Armin, an introduction by 18th Century theater scholar Jean Marsden, and a high quality facsimile of the original play as published in 1823.

Trade Paperback ISBN-13: 978-0615663166 Paperback $11.95
Also Available in **Kindle eBook** (without facsimile)

MORECLACKE PUBLISHING

Also Recommended

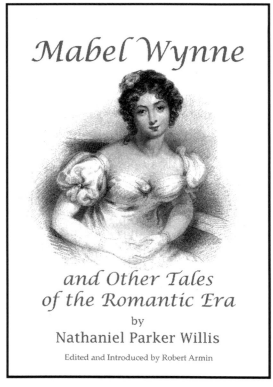

Mabel Wynne

and Other Tales of the Romantic Era

by

Nathaniel Parker Willis

Edited and Introduced by Robert Armin

Mabel Wynne and Other Tales of the Romantic Age is a selection of short romantic fiction and poems by Nineteenth Century American writer, editor, journalist and international travel correspondent, Nathaniel Parker Willis (1806-1867), newly edited and introduced by novelist Robert Armin. Beautifully illustrated with rare etchings and decorative drop cap lettering all reproduced from vintage books of the period. Also included are five essays by Willis on the American Woman, as originally published in the *New York Mirror* and *The Home Journal*.

Trade Paperback ISBN-13: 978-1499187229 Paperback $9.95
Also Available in Kindle eBook and Audiobook

MORECLACKE PUBLISHING

Made in the USA
Middletown, DE
08 April 2015